PAUSE

KYLIE SCOTT

NEW YORK TIMES BESTSELLING AUTHOR

Cover Design: By Hang Le
Cover Photograph: Michelle Lancaster @lanefotograf
Interior Book Design: Champagne Book Design

ISBN: 978-0-6484573-1-2

PLAYLIST

"Bust Your Windows" by Jazmine Sullivan

"Mad Woman" by Taylor Swift

"Wildflowers" by Tom Petty

"Feeling Good" by Nina Simone

"killing boys" by Halsey

"Adore You" by Harry Styles

"Beyond" by Leon Bridges

"Jackie and Wilson" by Hozier

PAUSE

PROLOGUE

"WHAT'S WRONG?" I ASK. OR TRY TO ASK. ONLY MY throat is sore and dry, so my voice barely rises above a whisper. Not even swallowing seems to help. "Mom?"

She wipes away the tears in a rush. "Sweetheart."

Everything in the strange white room seems hazy and insubstantial. I blink repeatedly, trying to clear my view. There's a vase of fading pink roses sitting on a small side table and I'm hooked up to a drip along with an array of machines. My body is one long, dull, horrible ache. What the hell happened?

"You were in an accident," says Dad, answering the question I hadn't yet asked. He rises from a chair in the corner of the room. "Do you remember?"

Before I can answer, Mom's there with her tremulous smile. "You've woken up before, but never for long. You keep going back to sleep."

None of this makes sense. "What . . ."

"The doctor told us that we have to ask you how you're feeling and what you can remember," she says.

"W-wait," I stutter. "Where's Ryan?"

They share a worried glance.

1

"What's going on?" I ask.

"What do you remember?" Mom perches on the edge of the bed. "How do you feel?"

"Can you move your fingers and toes?" asks Dad.

"I feel confused and frustrated." I stop to swallow again. Still not helping. "But yes, my fingers and toes are fine."

Mom rushes to fetch a plastic cup full of water with a straw sticking out for me. I try to take it slow, try to just sip it, but it tastes so good.

"I don't remember an accident," I admit once I'm finished.

"Another car hit you and you lost control."

They both wait for me to react. For recognition to strike. But I've got nothing. "When?"

"Let's wait for the doctor," says Mom, wringing her hands.

"Just tell me. Please."

"It's the fourteenth of February." Dad straightens his tie in a rare show of nerves. "That's the date today."

I frown. "No. No, that can't be."

Mom nods, adamant.

"What?" I ask, incredulous.

"Seven Months. Yes," says Dad.

"It's a long time to be in a coma. No one thought you'd wake up." Mom balls up a Kleenex in her hands. "The doctors said . . . it doesn't matter what they said now. You're a medical miracle. I knew you'd be okay. My daughter's a fighter."

Holy shit.

While none of this makes sense, it's all too real to be a joke. Not that my parents have much of a sense of humor. But there's nothing false in my mother's pained eyes. The last thing I can remember was it being July and we were at home planning a barbeque. Only a summer storm hit on my way to the store, the first rain in over a month. Then nothing.

Seven months of my life just gone. Halloween, Thanksgiving, Christmas, and New Year's. Summer, autumn, and winter. A whole half a year. It can't be. It isn't possible.

My brain won't cooperate and even attempting to lift my hand is a strain. It doesn't look any different, but I'm so damn weak and locked up. And where's my engagement ring, my wedding band? Guess they took them off me for security reasons, but still. I don't like it.

"Where's Ryan?" I ask again.

Dad flinches.

Mom turns away.

"Where is my husband?" This time my voice is trembling. There was no one else in the car with me. Ryan stayed home to sweep the deck and clean the grill. To get everything ready. I don't remember anyone being in the passenger seat. But then I don't remember an accident either, just some vague shadowy dreams. This is hell.

"Oh, sweetheart," says Mom, eyes glossy with unshed tears.

"He isn't . . ." I can't say the word *dead*. I don't want to even think it. "What happened?"

"He's on his way." Dad slips his cell phone back into his pants pocket, all while avoiding my eyes. "Just try and stay calm, Anna. Getting all upset about the situation won't help anything."

Despite my father's words, my breath comes faster. A full-on panic attack all of about two seconds away. Not easy to do from a prone position, but I'm giving it my best damn shot. "What the hell is going on?"

CHAPTER ONE

THREE MONTHS LATER...

L eif Larsen lives in a big old brown brick building with a sprawling dogwood out front in a cool urban neighborhood. No one answers when I press the buzzer. But according to the details on the scrap of paper the nurse gave me, I've got the right place.

What to do?

The rational response would be to give up and go home. Because hiding out in my childhood bedroom has worked out great so far (and this would be sarcasm). It's been months since I left the house for anything other than a medical appointment. Weeks since I've heard from any friends. Right on cue, my cell buzzes inside my tan Coach purse. I don't bother to look. Mom requests proof of life every hour on the hour. Not even dinner at the country club can distract her, apparently. Her parental concern for me is well past claustrophobic.

My hand clenches the iron railing against a gust of unseasonably warm evening wind. It's been a while since I stopped using a mobility aid, but things can still feel tricky. The whole damn world does, if I'm being honest. So many things I took for granted have now been turned upside down.

This is the problem with living the supposed dream. With having an airtight plan for your life. Meet Prince Charming and marry him. Find the perfect job. Only problem is, if something goes wrong, when reality smacks you upside the head and sends you reeling, then there's no system for putting the pieces back together. There's no Plan B because it never occurred to you that you'd need one. A lack of imagination on my part, perhaps.

A motorcycle pulls up to the curb and it's like everything happens in slow motion. Something about this long, lean man just makes time want to stand still. A denim-clad leg is swung over the back of the iron beast. A helmet is removed and shoulder-length hair tumbles free. High cheekbones and perfect lips are framed by stubble and all I can do is stare.

I don't know if I'm intimidated or turned on or what.

"Can I help y . . ." he begins. There's the faintest spark of recognition in his eyes.

I continue to stand there frozen.

"Fuck me," he mutters, stalking closer. His gaze slides over me from top to toe, lingering on the small scars on my left cheek from the glass. There's no attempt made to hide his curiosity. "It's really you."

Nichelle the nurse described him as being a nice young man. Nothing more. Certainly nothing that would prepare me for this. And I dispute "nice." Ripped denim, battered leather, and a Harley-Davidson motorbike are not *nice*.

"Never seen you conscious before," he says, getting even closer.

I just blink.

5

From beneath the collar and cuffs of his leather jacket emerge colorful tattoos. Lots of them. Blue waves and black letters. Red flames and white flowers. The man is a walking, talking piece of art. My parents would be horrified. Ryan too, for that matter. Not that any of their opinions matter. I need to forge my own path. Go my own way.

"How did you find me?" he asks with a faint frown.

"Oh. Ah." I smooth down the front of my pale blue midi-length linen summer dress. My dark hair is slicked back in a low ponytail and my makeup is simple but perfect. It's nice having some things I can control. "One of the nurses from the ICU told me about you and I wanted to come say thank you. But maybe an apology would be more in order?"

For a moment he pauses, then he asks, "Do you want to come in?"

Good question. The fact is, I don't know. Nor do I know how to do this. Something made obvious when my mouth opens, but nothing comes out. So much nothing for such a length of time that it's beyond embarrassing. Dammit. Whatever it is I came here looking for, it wasn't this. Him. Whatever.

"We've never properly met, have we?" He holds out his big hand. "Hi, I'm Leif."

"Anna."

While I'm tentative, he shows no such reserve. Strong, warm fingers enfold my own stiff and cold ones. There's no attempt at a dominating handshake or groping. He gives my hand a squeeze, just the one gentle squeeze, before setting me free.

"I'd say it's nice to meet you, but that would be weird." He grins conspiratorially and oh my God. Everything low in my stomach wakes up and takes notice. Shame on my lady parts, but the chemical pull of the man is ridiculous. It takes me a minute to remember that I'm a married woman. Mostly. Well, somewhat anyway. I certainly have no business smiling at him like I am. My life is messed up enough without adding a crush. Perhaps it's in reaction to me, I don't know, but the mirth disappears and his gaze becomes serious. A little bleak even. "I still have nightmares about that day, you know?"

"I'm sorry."

"Not your fault."

"I shouldn't have come."

"Don't, Anna. Don't look like that. I didn't tell you to hurt you or make you uncomfortable. I was just . . . sharing." His expression changes again, a more subdued smile taking the place of the brief hint of trauma. Then he suddenly winks at me all flirty like. I don't know how to react. I can barely keep up. The man is a whirlwind. "Want to come in and have a beer with me?"

"Are you sure?"

"Yes."

"I just . . . I don't want to remind you of things you'd rather—"

"I want you to come inside. I wouldn't have asked otherwise."

A drink with a pretty wild man that I have a strange sort of history with or a swift return to safety and boredom? I don't overthink it. I don't even hesitate. "Then yes, Leif. I'd love to."

The police report states that when I lost control of my car, a man on a motorcycle was forced off the road to avoid impact. This was after I was hit by the other vehicle, but before I hit the tree. While the other driver fled the scene, the man on the motorcycle sustained a compound fracture to his right arm and was transported to the same hospital as me for treatment. The man who sat by my hospital bed every night reading to me. Until he stopped showing up.

None of this explains, however, why he doesn't own a single piece of furniture in his condo, besides a king-size mattress. Not a single thing hangs on the blank white walls. And the mattress is just lying there, in the center of the open kitchen/dining/living space. There are two small bedrooms, but he's not bothering to use either one of them. The mattress is covered with rumpled sheets and discarded pillows. My brain is far too happy to imagine all the obscene acts he might have participated in on that bed. It's disturbing to say the least. Porn thoughts aren't my usual go-to.

"You're probably more of a white wine drinker, huh?" He pops the top on a can of Swish Bissell Brothers beer and passes it to me.

"This is fine. Thank you."

After downing a mouthful of his own IPA, he gives the mostly empty room a glance. "Only got the place a couple of months back. Still working on furniture and stuff."

I nod in acknowledgment, my grip on my purse strap tightening. It's kind of my safety blanket. But he's had months to get organized. Good Lord. Medical bills would have done their damage, but still. The place is all but empty. A hollow shell. Not a home.

"Maybe we should have gone out," he says.

"It's fine."

He lifts himself up onto the kitchen counter and looks down at me, swinging his legs like a child. "You know, you keep saying the word 'fine.' But I can basically see the tic in your eye from my lack of a sofa and ottoman."

I am not amused.

"An armoire and a side table too, maybe. A couple of lamps for some mood lighting." He shrugs off his leather jacket. The short sleeves of his gray tee reveal even more ink along with the ripple of a whole lot of lean muscles. I don't let my gaze linger on the gnarled and jagged pink scar on his upper arm. And meanwhile there's a gleam in Leif's amber eyes, one that suggests he's enjoying himself way too much. "Don't even get me started on the lack of suitable glassware and drinks coasters. Probably for the best that I don't have any furniture or we'd be leaving water marks everywhere. I don't even have a linen napkin to my name. I'm really not prepared for guests at all, am I?"

"You're teasing me."

"You're judging me."

Shit. "I don't mean to," I say, subdued. Horrified at being called out.

Coming here was such a bad idea. He's a veritable stranger and we have nothing in common. Nothing good, at any rate. Then there's the part where I've been standing for too long. I hate the lingering weakness. My therapist says feelings of frustration and anger are to be expected. The accident has changed me. But mostly I'd just like to stop falling on my ass sometime soon.

"Come here," he says, jumping down with ease.

"What?"

"I'm going to lift you up onto the counter so you can get off your feet."

I just look at him.

"You need to sit, don't you? That's what the panicky face

and the shakes mean. Believe me, I know it all too well, having recently spent some time in rehab myself with the arm."

"Yes," I reluctantly admit.

He makes a come-hither motion with his hands. "It's okay, Anna. I'm actually sorry I don't have a sofa for you to sit on. May I help you?"

My options aren't great. The floor, the mattress, or this counter. And there's no way I can get up there on my own. "Thank you. Yes."

He's standing so close. The man must be a bit over six feet tall because I barely come up to his nose. Strong hands grip my waist and my breasts brush against his chest on the way up. Accidental, as evidenced by the slight widening of his eyes. As if he's never been up close to a bosom before. Please. And he smells ridiculously good. Clean, warm male sweat with a hint of spice. It verges on nirvana for a woman who hasn't had sex in almost a year. Not to mention the recognition that I am in fact a real live breathing person, with feminine wiles. The sensation that he's actually seeing me when I've felt nonexistent for so long is a heady thing. I've been a patient, a problem, everything but a strong, capable woman with a beating heart with wants and needs.

"Thanks," I say again, a little breathless this time.

"No problem." The way he stops and studies my face is weird. It's probably because I'm being weird. But finally, the odd moment ends, and he takes a step back. "Nice dress."

"Thank you."

"Tell me about yourself."

I counter with, "Nichelle said you visited me every night for a while in the hospital."

He sighs and crosses his arms. "I read to you at night for a few weeks. It's not a big deal."

"It kind of is. That was very sweet of you."

"Anna—"

"Don't," I say, harder than I mean to. "Don't diminish it. That you took the time to sit with me means a lot."

"Yeah. Well." He scratches his head. "Truth is, you were lousy company."

I bark out a surprised laugh. Then slap a hand over my mouth, because what an unholy loud noise.

Leif smiles behind his can of beer. "So come on, tell me about yourself."

"What do you want to know?"

"Start with the basics." He leans against the wall, one of his big-ass boots tapping out a beat in the silence. "Or surprise me. Whatever."

"Twenty-six. I was in hospitality, but that's all on hold." I shrug. "Grew up in Cape Elizabeth."

"Fancy neighborhood."

"If you say so. Only child. Went to college in New Hampshire." And that's basically me. "What about you?"

"Thirty-one. Local born and bred. Youngest of three sons. And I'm a tattoo artist."

I wrinkle my nose. "Wow."

"No ink for you, huh?"

"Not after all of the needles in the hospital." Not that it was a remote possibility beforehand, I mentally add. While I can appreciate how they look on him, I am nowhere near that interesting. Nor do I enjoy pain.

"Current relationship status?" he asks, gaze dropping to my

bare hand. I'm sure it doesn't mean anything. Just your standard heteronormative reaction.

"Um." This question causes an even mix of awkward and painful. I should be used to it by now, but oh well. "It's complicated. Well . . . separated. Yeah."

"Right. I, um . . ." His mouth opens, then closes, as if he's thought better of whatever he was going to say. Which is curious. "I'm sorry."

I just nod. To be honest, I'm still experiencing culture shock. My marriage and my husband were huge parts of my life. As they should be. Now it's like someone hit pause on all of that and I'm not sure how to feel or what to think. With my heart and mind in a permanent state of confusion, there's not much I can do. Not yet. And it's been like this for months. Betrayal has one hell of a sting and I can't get past the pain to come even remotely close to forgiveness. Not yet. Maybe not ever. Forget about putting my wedding ring back on any time soon.

"Favorite food?" he asks, moving on, thank goodness.

"Mexican."

"Excellent choice." He pulls his cell out of his back jeans pocket. "How hungry are you?"

"I could eat."

At this, he gives me the stink eye. "You know, women always say that all casual like and then they eat half of your food."

"Order enough and I won't eat half of your food." I hold back a smile. "It's that simple."

He sighs. "I get the distinct feeling that nothing about you is simple. But I'm going to feed you anyway. How do you feel about tacos?"

"I love them."

"Carne asada?"

"Would be great."

"Queso and chips?"

"Please. And Mexican corn if they have it."

"They do. Okay," he says, busy with his cell. "We're set. You know, you're the first person I've had come visit me here outside of family."

"Really? Why?"

A shrug. "I don't know. Just busy, I guess."

I take another sip of beer. Which is when I realize I feel comfortable here, and I'm even having a good time. My first in a while. "Let me pay for half."

"No. I'm buying you dinner. It's a done deal." He tosses his cell on the counter. "Next time you can pay."

"There's going to be a next time?" I ask.

"Sure," he says, fetching himself another beer out of the fridge. "We've already had our bonding moment. I watched you get cut out of your car and everything. I was even holding your hand for a while until the paramedics arrived on the scene. So yeah, we survived a traumatic event together. More than the other guy who caused the accident and took off without helping can say."

"Am I a bad person for fervently hoping that God smites him?"

"Nope. I got a titanium plate and eight screws in my arm. Not my idea of a good time." He winces at the memory. "That compound fracture could have ended my career. Let alone what he did to you."

I raise my brows. "Subdural hematoma, hemorrhagic contusions, a dislocated shoulder, and five broken ribs."

"Exactly."

"How is your arm? Is it okay now?"

"Eh. Pretty much. I had okay insurance, so I didn't come out of it too badly. And I can tell when it's going to rain now, which is always handy," he says, his expression darkening. "That was a fucked-up thing, that accident. We're lucky to be alive."

"Very true. You didn't see the other car?"

He winces. "It was a silver sedan. Beyond that, I've got nothing. I sure as hell wish I'd seen the driver or the license plate or something useful."

I take another sip of beer, thinking it all over. My cell buzzes again inside my purse. I will not look at it. I won't.

"You need to get that?" he asks, settling himself on the floor.

I shake my head. "No. It's my mother. I appreciate her caring, but she's gotten clingy. I'm trying to deprogram her back to a manageable level."

"Fair enough."

"Just because I'm a little fragile doesn't mean I'm no longer an adult," I say, and boy do I sound cranky. On the verge of ranting, even. Not good.

"How are you doing with all of that, if you don't mind me asking?"

"Better than I was at first. I had to learn to walk and feed myself all over again. And there's a lot more rehabilitation in front of me."

He just nods.

"It's unlikely I'll be running anytime soon."

"Running sucks. My brother and his wife live next door and he makes me go with him all of the damn time."

"I have to be honest, I'm not really missing that part of it. Though it would be nice to have the option."

"Any white tunnel moments? Did you go toward the light and see your life flash before your eyes?" he asks.

"No." I shake my head. "Some weird dreams about spooky shadows, though. I think it was just the difference between day and night. Nothing interesting."

He leans his head back against the wall, watching me thoughtfully. "If I can say one thing on the subject of your mom . . ."

"Okay."

"I was only in the hospital for a few days. Long enough for them to operate and put some screws in to hold my arm together," he says. "But it was enough to see what was going on around you. The way your people were taking turns to stay with you. So you wouldn't wake up and have no one there, you know?"

I nod because I do know. Mom and Dad don't like to talk about it, but Ryan was only too willing to discuss all he'd done. Sharing the many and varied details in an attempt to prove himself the dutiful husband. The hours he spent by my bedside. The sacrifices he made. The long, lonely hours, et cetera. Poor Ryan.

Mind you, waking from a long vegetative state is no small feat. That the odds were against me was made abundantly clear by posts on my Facebook page. Old stories about me. Thoughts and prayers. Messages of loss like I'd already died. There was even a "rest in peace." No wonder Ryan gave up on me—just about everyone else had. Though those others hadn't stood up in front of a preacher and taken vows.

Anyway.

"Your mom took the night shifts," Leif continues. "She didn't mind me sitting with you because it meant she could go grab a coffee or go for a walk or whatever without worrying. Even though the first time we met she looked at me like I was there to steal her purse."

"I come from a judgmental family, apparently."

"You upper-middle-class suburbanites, you're all the same." He winks at me. "But, Anna, she was a wreck. It's probably not my place to say this, but that woman would do anything for you."

I sigh. "I know."

"Despite being a wreck, she was all over your treatment, grilling the doctors and nurses, getting all up in their faces if she wasn't sure something they were doing was best for her baby girl. It was a beautiful thing to see."

"You're making me feel like a bad daughter."

He downs a mouthful of beer. "No one could blame you for being pissed about the situation. It's got to be a huge adjustment."

"I had to move back in with them when I got out of the hospital for various reasons and . . . it's been an adjustment for everyone, I think."

"My mother is a wonderful woman. But she does have white carpet and a special day of the week for doing laundry," he says. "So trust me, I understand. There's no way I could move back home."

I give him a glum smile and look around to buy myself time. To put my thoughts in order. It's really quite a nice condo. Older, with character. The kitchen could use some work and I'm guessing the bathroom is similar. But still. The high ceiling and wood-framed windows have charm.

He clears his throat. "What about your friends, they being supportive?"

"Oh. That too is complicated." And while I don't particularly want to say more, he just waits patiently for my explanation. "Most of the people I was close to . . . their lives have kind of moved on. Or I can no longer keep up. I get so easily exhausted."

"That must suck."

I nod. "Mom insists on driving me to all of my medical appointments, so we spend a lot of time together. She's had to cut back on church and her Scrabble group to fit it all in."

He says nothing.

"The truth is, I hate putting her out all of the time. I feel like an inconvenience in my own life."

His gaze is soft and sympathetic. "Anna . . ."

Oh, God. I'm the worst. The absolute ruling queen of negative losers. "And then for fun, I whine at hot guys."

At this, he immediately perks up. "You think I'm hot?"

"What? No."

"You said *hot*. I distinctly heard the word *hot*."

"I know, right? Would it kill you to turn the AC on?"

He snorts. "Very funny."

"Thanks."

Despite not having flirted in forever, it would seem I haven't lost the knack entirely. It's heartening. There's also not even one iota of guilt inside me. So there. Not that I'm interested in or looking for more. My life is confusing enough right now. Nor would someone like Leif really be interested in me. I'm okay looking, but he's on a whole other level. Though the curious glance he gives me strays into titillation.

"You don't want the AC on, do you?" He raises a brow. "You'd tell me if you did, right?"

"No, I don't want it on. And yes, I would tell you." Despite my mother's belief in suffering in polite silence, I do not like to sweat. My milkmaid complexion turns lobster red and it all goes downhill from there.

"Good," he says, relaxing back against the wall once more. "I have a feeling this is the beginning of a beautiful friendship."

I take a deep breath. "Leif. Thank you. That's very kind of you. But I don't need your pity. I—"

"It's the resting bitch face that does it for me," he carries on, as if I hadn't said a word. "And who else is going to teach me all about linen napkins and matching silverware and the various stuff I now apparently require as a new homeowner?"

"Good sir, you mistake me for Martha Stewart on a bad day."

"Nuh." He grins. "You're way hotter."

Heat rushes into my face. Despite this, it's kind of impossible not to smile back at him. Not only is he pretty, but happiness is apparently contagious around this man. And that's exactly what I need right now.

He nods. "There we go. That's better."

Oh, God. Am I leading him on? "I'm still legally married, Leif."

"I said 'friends,' Anna. *Friends.*" He mock scowls, which is also exceptionally attractive. Dammit. "Don't go getting ahead of yourself."

"Sorry."

Then the doorbell buzzes and he's jumping to his feet. Our food must be here. Excellent, for I am hungry. I think what I came looking for here tonight was a life. A future or a way forward at least. And a new friend is a definite step in the right direction.

Except when he opens the door, shouting echoes down the hallway, and the voice is familiar. Painfully so.

"Where is my wife?" yells Ryan.

My face falls.

Meanwhile, Leif frowns before setting his jaw and striding off down the hall as if to do battle. *Oh shit.*

No, no, no. This is a disaster. I have to get out there and stop this. How to get down on my own? I roll onto my side, then onto my belly, then wiggle toward the edge of the counter. At long last, my dangling feet touch the ground and I'm a little rumpled but good to go.

I walk as fast as my feet will take me out the door, down the hallway, and out to the front of the building. Where a furious Ryan is facing off with a determined Leif, while a tall and also tattooed man watches on. There are no words for the pain of seeing my estranged husband. For having my current shitty reality hit home yet again. No wonder I avoid him whenever possible. It just hurts too much.

How the hell Ryan found me is answered by the cell in his hand. The phone tracker app. I'd completely forgotten about it. Back when our marriage was hale and hearty, it was useful to know where the other was. How far from home, or how close to the store. We both agreed to it and it was fine. But for him to be using it now, in this situation, makes my blood boil. Guess he rang the buzzer for a few different condos and that's why the other guy is out here. What a farce.

"I told you to stay away from her." Ryan jabs a finger into Leif's chest and oh my God. They've met before. That's why Leif stopped visiting me at the hospital. Ryan either got jealous or control freakish or a mean combination of both and warned him off. Holy cow. Never before has he behaved like this. At least, not that I'd ever seen. Like a bully. Like a spoiled child determined to get his way.

My stomach curdles at how loud and obnoxious he's being. I could honestly heave my beer into the bushes. He keeps darting looks at me out of the corner of his eye, like he's gauging how this whole scene is affecting me. My shoulders are slumped, beaten down by his words and his anger. As if I've already given in. Not okay. He doesn't get to show up here and make me the bad guy. And he doesn't get to shame me publicly, or otherwise, when I've done nothing wrong.

Leif stays silent.

"I fucking warned you," continues Ryan.

The other tattooed man stands there with his arms crossed, watching and waiting.

"Anna?" Ryan's hands are clenched into fists, hanging ready at his sides. "Are you okay?"

"Yes. Just deleting the app off my phone that you used to find me." I drop my cell back into my purse. "That won't be happening again."

He blinks in surprise. "I'm still your husband."

"And that gives you the right to stalk me?" I ask, indignant as all hell. "I don't think so. You're not my keeper. You don't own me."

"Anna, I love you."

"No," I say, my finger jabbing in his direction. "No, Ryan. You don't get to do what you did and call it love."

He lets out the heaviest of sighs. No man has ever been so poorly treated. Just ask him. It's like the stresses of my accident have created a second Ryan. A raging asshole Ryan. "Let me take you home. You look tired."

"I think she looks good," says Leif. Which is nice, but not helpful.

Ryan bristles. "Let me drive you back to your parents' place. Or you could come home with me. What do you think?"

"You don't care what I think. You know, I almost believed you were sincere about giving me space. About respecting my decision to take some time to figure things out." My laughter is a bitter thing. "You lie about everything these days. I don't even know who you are anymore."

"I was sincere. I *am* sincere." He swallows hard. "You're not thinking straight. You don't understand how—"

"Hard it was for you while I was in a coma. Yes, I know," I say. "So hard that you had to fuck one of my best friends."

"Anna," he chides. Ladies aren't supposed to swear. Especially not at him.

"He slept with your best friend while you were unconscious?" asks Leif. "Seriously?"

I nod.

"Ouch," says the other dude, whoever he is.

Ryan squares his shoulders. "This is none of your business. Either of you. This is between me and my wife."

Funny thing is, I don't feel like his wife anymore. I don't feel like a hell of a lot of anything. A blank piece of paper waiting for a new story to be written. The beginning of something with no future in sight. That's what it feels like to be me.

"Problem is," I say, "everyone knows because you were so damn careless that my mom walked in on you and her having a touching moment at my bedside. So not only did you cheat on me, but you were shitty at it!"

Ryan's mouth gapes at my outburst. But I do not apologize, nor will I calm down. Not this time, dammit.

My hands shake at my sides, but I am not some meek bitch to smile and nod and do his bidding. Not now. Not ever.

"Anna?" Leif is asking me what I want to do. It's nice that someone here still thinks I'm a capable adult and not a broken thing in need of handling.

"You shouldn't have come here," I say, placing a hand on the railing to hold myself steady. "I mean . . . my husband and one of my closest friends. Not only my whole damn life, but some of the most important relationships in it, got fucked while I was unconscious. Every time I think I've got a handle on it the whole thing just slaps me in the face all over again. Do you have any idea how that feels? To be made to feel so small and stupid by the actions of people who are supposed to love you?"

"You're being unreasonable," mutters my husband like he's dealing with an irate child.

Truth is, I've been pretty sedate about things until now. Apart from crying for the first month and hiding out in my room the rest of the time. Maybe I've just been reluctant to get loud and messy in public. To delve deep into the nitty-gritty of the situation. Practicing denial and hiding from shit has been so much more helpful. Not. Guess this showdown has been coming for a while. And it's his fault for showing up here and forcing things.

My hands shake with righteous fury. "Ryan, you need to leave. Now."

He opens his mouth, but no.

"Now," I repeat.

He stomps off, climbs into his new company Chevrolet Silverado, and slams the door shut. *Give me strength.*

I just wilt, my chin sitting on my chest. "I'm so sorry."

"Not your fault," says Leif. "Hey. It's okay. Really."

The other guy disappears inside without another word.

Meanwhile, I'm about to burst into tears like an idiot. There have probably been more embarrassing situations in the history of space and time, I just can't think of any right now. Thing is, I was having a nice evening. I was doing all right. I was going to eat Mexican corn, dammit. Then Ryan had to come at me with his hypocritical possessive bullshit.

I could honestly scream, but I don't. "He's why you stopped coming to read to me."

Leif just nods. And it's the pity that kills me. The sorrow in his gaze and lines set in his face. I can't do it. I can't face him like this.

"I'm so sorry. About everything. Him turning up here and . . . I'm sorry." And I get out of there as fast I can.

CHAPTER TWO

THE FIRST SIGN THAT SOMETHING IS WRONG IS THE silence. It's so complete the house seems to echo with it. No music. No chatter. Nothing. Mom hates the quiet and her car is here, so I know she's home. It's been over a week since I visited Leif and my outlook has not particularly improved. Nor will it be improving in the next short while. Because there's a bump like someone knocking into a piece of furniture and it's followed by a giggle.

Oh, God. She wouldn't have. Surely.

Then my worst nightmare comes true. Assorted friends and acquaintances leap out from behind various objects shouting, "Happy birthday!"

Fuck no. Kill me now.

I paste a smile on my face as Mom steps out from the kitchen. Her grin is huge and hopeful. People hug me while someone presses a glass of champagne into my hand. There's Zola, Lucy, Cho, and James from the inn where I used to work. My old neighbors, Julia and Will. Erin and her girlfriend Angie from the tennis club where I used to play. And last but not least, Briar from college. Thank goodness she's here.

No wonder Mom said she wouldn't be available to pick me up. And I look a mess, having only braided my wet hair after showering post hydrotherapy. Same goes for my pair of denim cutoffs and an old blouse that are more yard work than surprise birthday party. Glam I am not.

Forget pink champagne, I require hard liquor.

The team from the inn hangs back after offering felicitations. There's a nervous sort of energy to them. Fair enough, considering their boss is my former best friend Celine, the husband fucker. No wonder I no longer have a job. As if I could ever go back there. Us both sleeping with the same man makes for quite the conflict of interest in the workplace. Not that I've slept with Ryan, or anyone, in the last ten or so months. How awkward.

My old neighbors are likewise an awkward situation waiting to happen. Any and all previous socializing was done as part of a couple. Picnics, potlucks, things like that. We were like mirror images of each other. Two upwardly mobile professional around-thirty-year-old couples. And I am now distinctly uncoupled, out of work, and have mobility issues. No wonder I didn't want a party. Not that anyone asked me. Hear me whine.

One close friend of mine in days of yore was Ryan's sister Natasha. But she's been suspiciously quiet since I woke up. It's amazing how people prefer to disappear over facing their own foibles. Or their family's foibles. I'm certainly not immune to engaging in this behavior, but it doesn't make it any easier to be on the receiving end.

Although Mom has been cautious with the guest list, everyone here knows that my husband banged one of my best friends. Awesome. Whelp, no point in avoiding my guests. I square my shoulders and face the crowd with a smile.

The question is, who are you when your job, your relationship, and one of your best friends are gone? I'm adrift in a sea of what the fuck. I'd like to think that Celine will come crawling on her hands and knees, begging me to return to working at the inn. But the fact is, I'm not irreplaceable. And they've had over half a year to replace me. At this point, I doubt I'll even be getting a well-deserved glowing reference.

"So good to see you!" Erin smacks a kiss on my cheek.

"You too," I say.

Angie grabs my hand and presses it to her bulging belly. "Say hello."

"Hello, little one," I say dutifully. It's impossible not to be happy for Erin and Angie. There's such an air of joy to them, a feeling of growth. They also don't give a crap that Ryan isn't standing at my side. What a relief. I don't know them very well, but what I do know I like.

"You look distinctly uncomfortable," says Briar. She's a short, curvy black woman with killer style and a law degree. "Is it physical or emotional?"

"Both."

"Ah. Sit down and drink up then."

"Good idea."

We grab some chairs in the corner of the dining room, facing the table laden with tastefully wrapped gifts and small decorative plates of appetizers. Hummus on slices of cucumber, fruit and prosciutto bites, and a cheese board. Mom believes in healthy food to speed my recovery and protein to build up my muscle mass. To balance this, there's also a beautiful cake with buttercream frosting surrounded by berries. When she passes by with a plate of goodies, I grab her spare hand. "Thanks for this."

She delicately snorts in a ladylike manner. "Please, you hate it. But life goes on. I wasn't going to just let you ignore your birthday. Happy twenty-seventh, sweetheart."

"Thank you."

And despite giving my shabby outfit a skeptical glance, she just nods. God bless Mom. She can't help herself. We really are every bit as judgmental as Leif says. And there I go again, thinking about him. It's not helpful. Though at least it doesn't hurl me into a pit of despair like contemplating my husband does.

Interestingly, Dad isn't here. But Dad hates any socializing that doesn't take place on the golf course. Perhaps I'm more like my antisocial father these days. Though I'm never going to play golf.

At any rate, Leif was right: my mom in action is a beautiful thing. I have deep thoughts about Leif more often than I should. I'd been so embarrassed by Ryan showing up and trying to start a fight that I got out of there pronto after he left. No one needs that kind of drama in their life, or the person who invited it in.

On the other hand, knowing someone supportive who'd survived the same accident was nice. Comforting. Even if it was brief. Perhaps I'll find the courage to see him again. Maybe. In the meantime, I'm going to stop thinking about him. Right now.

"I should go put on something more suitable," I say, not moving an inch.

Briar crosses her legs. "Catch your breath first."

"If I'd known this was happening I'd have at least shaved my legs."

"Never mind. I hear the Viking look is in this season."

"Nice." I laugh. "Are you suggesting I could braid them?"

Her brows rise. "Now that would be something."

Over by the front windows, the group from the inn is huddled together. Lots of side-eye going on. Lots of whispering. Ugh.

"Ignore them," says my friend.

"Have you heard from her lately?" I ask.

Briar, Celine, and I met as neighboring dorm buddies and moved up to sharing an apartment in our senior year. Many a fun time was had. I met Ryan when we were freshmen. We've been together ever since. And it wasn't perfect, but it was good. There were times we had to work at it. Times when we had to fight for it. But we always did and I thought we'd be together forever. Right up until we weren't. Talk about life slapping you in the face.

"Not since I told her exactly what I thought of her so-called unfortunate lapse of judgment. If she expected me to be understanding, then she was severely disappointed." Briar takes another sip of her drink. "I don't care how scared and exhausted either of them were. You don't open your legs to comfort your still very much alive friend's husband."

"Hmm."

"What does *hmm* mean?"

I sigh. "She texted me again the other day. I didn't respond. It was the usual, 'We're both so sorry. Neither of us meant to hurt you. Please try and understand. We still love you and care about you very much.' I think it's the 'us' and the 'we' that aggravates me. The continued implied coupledom. The unity. He's my fucking husband. Or he was. I don't know what he is now."

Briar just shakes her head.

"He was so sorry, you know? He even cried," I say. "I can't remember the last time he cried. When his grandma died, maybe?"

"And?"

"I've tried to understand. I mean, it must have been hell for him, going through all of that." My shoulders slump. "I've tried to put myself in his position and imagine if it was him on that bed and me not knowing if he'd ever wake up. And even if he did wake up, not knowing if he'd be the same person."

She sighs.

"I still wouldn't turn to his damn friend," I add. "I wouldn't disrespect him that way."

"Exactly." Briar tries for a smile, but it doesn't quite work. "She always did use too many exclamation points when she messaged or texted."

"Ugh. Yeah. Wait, are we being unnecessarily petty?"

"I debate your use of 'unnecessary.'"

"Lady, you make me laugh. You know, he's been pushing for me to move back home and do couple's counseling," I say, staring off at nothing. "But I'm not sure we can come back from this. How can I possibly trust him again?"

She takes my hand in a warm grip. "Anna, I'm going to send you the name of a local divorce lawyer that I recommend. My cousin used her a few years back."

I pause.

"No pressure. Just in case. It's always good to have a backup plan."

"Okay. Thanks."

Deep breath in, slow breath out. My parents have been married for thirty years and I can't even manage two. The thought of taking this final step is . . . *shit*. Not just failing so spectacularly, but having everyone know. It shouldn't matter, but it does. It's like there's a crack inside of me widening a little more every day and out pours all of the hope and love and everything that ever meant anything to me. My marriage has been upended and my reality has been reset—I can't keep up.

"Is this why you're back in town for a few days?" I ask.

"That, birthday cake, and the annual sale at Braun's Books. You know I never miss that." She grins. "You needed to know your options. And that you're not alone."

"Thank you."

"You could come back to New York with me." She taps her elbow gently against mine. "Start over in the big city, away from all of this nonsense. What do you say?"

"That's a big move. I don't know."

"Could be fun. Even if it was just for a little while."

"Yeah, but do you remember how I used to drive you crazy when we shared a room back in college?"

"You color coded my wardrobe."

"I told you not to give me the edible."

She laughs. "I thought it might relax you. Little did I know that your version of relaxation is organizing someone else's life."

"I'm not that bad."

A snort from the lady. "I beg to differ."

"Well, my control freak ways have had a setback. Rest assured."

"Hmm," says Briar. "I have yet to see any proof. You look pretty good to me."

I slump back in the seat. "The proof is my life. My whole being now is . . . I don't even know the word. *Boom* maybe? *Kapow* perhaps?"

"Your life blew up, huh?"

"Just a little."

"As long as you're not dwelling on it and feeling sorry for yourself," says Briar.

Now it's my turn to laugh. I'm such a basic bitch these days.

Suddenly, I hear a commotion in the foyer. Mom's mouth is a perfect 'o' and Ryan stands there with a bouquet of long-stemmed red roses. Once again, turning up without an invitation. There's no way Mom would have given him one. But he knows if he just shows up, she doesn't know how to say no.

"Quelle surprise," says Briar.

Cho gasps. James already has his cell in hand. Celine is going to know about this in approximately two seconds, given the speed at which James's thumbs are moving.

That's the other thing about all of this—I don't quite believe it's over between them. That it was a one-time thing. A mistake. Because whether or not they're currently having sex, I think they're still involved on some level. Each and every time I see my husband, the guilt in his eyes seems to have risen. Same too the resentment over how difficult I'm being about an unfortunate accident. His words, not mine. And he's not referring to the car accident. Hell no.

"Happy birthday," Ryan says, then smiles all hopeful like and bends down by my chair. He's so handsome. Dark hair and blue eyes. Tall and strong. Everything I thought I could ever want. But I don't see him the same way anymore. The trust and friendship are missing. The love and fidelity. He threw it all away. "These are for you, honey."

"They're beautiful."

"Can we talk for a minute?" he asks. "In private?"

"Sure." The weight of every eye in the room rests heavy on my shoulders. "Let's go into the kitchen."

31

He frowns briefly, as if he was hoping for my bedroom.

"Can you pass me a vase, please?" I point to the top shelf in the pantry. The blooms are big and bold and a perfect dark red. I fetch the shears to cut the ribbon holding them together and Ryan sets the vase beside me. "Thank you."

"Your mother didn't invite me, but I heard about it from Julia and Will." His voice is tight and tense, leaving no doubt that my mom has done him wrong.

I just nod. Given the situation, she did what she thought was best. I'm not making excuses for her just to appease him. Bet he wishes my dad were here. Dad's his biggest fan and can always be depended upon to make him feel welcome—which made for some uncomfortable situations over the past few months. It also does nothing to address the situation, being that if I don't want him here, then I should ask him to go. Only I'm not sure what I want, what with being a heart betrayed and divided, so here we are.

"We need to talk," he says.

"I'm listening."

It's hard to look at him. Like he's a stranger, unknown and untrustworthy. Guess he feels the same way because his jaw shifts and his gaze wanders. To the fridge, along the counter, up to the window. Everywhere but at me.

As if there hasn't been enough furtive and shady behavior already. The apology for following me to Leif's was grudging and half-hearted at best. Made only after I refused to answer his calls or respond to his texts for several days. This is what we've become . . . this ruin. Though he doesn't have a hair out of place. His white button-down shirt is immaculate. Same goes for his pinstripe pants. No tie. He would have removed it in the car after he left work. I can just picture him tugging it free and casting it aside. The tension in his broad shoulders easing the farther he drives away from work. I know him so well, but none of that seems to matter these days.

I fill the vase with water and lift the first rose. No thorns. The florist must have dealt with them. Too bad someone can't do that for my life. "What is it, Ryan?"

"You haven't heard . . . never mind. Of course you haven't."

I frown. "What are you talking about?"

His face is both empty and set. Giving nothing away. "Celine's pregnant."

Everything stops.

"Anna . . ."

I take a deep breath in and let it out slowly, trying to pull myself together. It's like I've been sucker punched. My brain is reeling, the information refusing to sink in, to make sense. "I really wasn't expecting that."

He moves to come closer but I hold up a hand to stop him. "Please, honey. It doesn't have to affect you and me."

There's a stabbing pain inside of me. My heart, I think. Like the last piece of it is breaking, shattering into smithereens. I ran out of tears a while back. Our love has become this brittle thing I couldn't fix even if I wanted to. That's the truth. "We were going to try for a baby this year," I say in a broken voice.

A little human, half him, half me. A family of our own. It might have been hormones, but the thought used to thrill and delight me. And now he's done that with Celine. A bridesmaid at our wedding. One of my oldest and most trusted friends.

"We still can, if you want," he says.

I wrinkle my nose. "Holy shit. Are you serious?"

"Yes." And he is, God help him. "There's no need for that kind of language."

"How far along is she?"

His lips morph into a thin line. Which is answer enough.

"Four months," I say helpfully. "This is where you say 'four months'—and tell me that she's just starting to show. Because you swore you only had sex the one time, remember? A terrible, horrible mistake that just happened once. You remember the story. I'd been unconscious for six months. The doctors had just suggested flicking off the switch and you turned to each other for consolation. So Celine should be four months pregnant."

Only she's not, she's less than that. I can see it all over his face. The last little bit of hope inside of me dies. It sucks to be right. I wanted our marriage to be stronger than this. For our love to mean more than this. But it isn't and it doesn't and I'm done. You can only volunteer to get knocked down so many times unless you enjoy living on your knees.

I cross to the sink, taking the flowers with me.

"Anna—"

Mom's waste disposal roars to life at the flick of the switch. She really should get it fixed. It clunks and clatters and sounds like it's coming apart. More than loud enough to drown out the worst of my husband's useless bullshit protestations that I've heard a thousand times. How he still loves me. How he's sorry. How he never meant for this to happen. How we can still make this right if I would just let him fix things. Only some things can't be fixed. Shouldn't be fixed.

Other people come to the kitchen door to see what's happening, but I ignore them. Awkward and embarrassing and whatever—I don't care. If we have an audience, so what? I haven't had control over any other aspect of my life lately. Let them see my meltdown in all its furious shambolic glory. Let them witness the final death throes of my supposed great love. It sure makes for one hell of a dramatic birthday. Forget party games, spectacle is the go. It's his own fault for coming here and doing this now. The idiot.

One at a time, I feed the beautiful, glorious roses into the machine. It churns and crunches and gurgles and grinds them into a gooey pulp. And I don't stop until every last rose is gone. It's cathartic, really. Satisfying. Like some weird piece of domestic performance art. And I'm not even artistic.

The silence rings in my ears when I finally turn off the waste disposal. "I want a divorce."

For once, Ryan doesn't say a thing.

Larsen and Sons Tattoo Parlor is only a few blocks away from Leif's condo in the same cool urban area with busy streets. Purse on my shoulder and bottle of single-malt scotch in hand, I head inside. The buzz of the drill sets my teeth on edge, but everything is clean and orderly. Not even my mother could find fault with the place. There's an old grandfather clock and a green chaise. Lots of framed drawings on the walls. And rock 'n' roll plays over the sound system. Some old Tom Petty song, I think.

At the counter stands a woman with beautiful dark curly hair and a whole lot of ink on her umber skin. She seems flustered and sets the phone down as she asks, "Can I help you?"

"No," a familiar voice yells from farther back. "But I can."

The woman raises a brow and gives him a questioning look over her shoulder.

"I'm here to see Leif," I say with a hesitant smile.

He's standing beside a massage-type table giving me his devil-may-care grin. Or maybe it's the scotch he's smiling at.

My hands shake from nerves. "Hi."

"You come bearing gifts."

"Yes, I do."

There's a large man with gray hair laid out on the table in front of Leif with a fresh tattoo happening on his left arm. He turns his head and looks me over with interest. Same goes for the other tattooist working at the back table on a woman. Only this man isn't a stranger. He's the one who stood watching while Ryan tried to pick a fight with Leif. The one from in front of the condo that day. Awesome. This is so embarrassing.

"You're turning pink," says Leif, head cocked with obvious interest. "What does it mean when you turn pink?"

Oh, God.

"Don't be an ass," says the woman with the fabulous hair. "Come on through, you're fine. I'm Tessa."

"Anna. Nice to meet you."

Tessa pulls out a chair close to Leif and directs me to it. I like Tessa. She takes in the collection of small pink scars on my face and the one dissecting the edge of my upper lip, but doesn't dwell on them. I put on makeup, but didn't go overboard trying to cover them. They're part of me now. Time to accept and move on. My face is different, my body is changed, and my life is altered. It's not the end of the world. It just feels like it sometimes. As for how I feel about Leif, I'm still deciding. The other dude keeps working on the lady's back, sneaking looks at me. Fair enough. I'm a little curious about who he is too. Without another word, Tessa heads out the back door. I'm kind of sorry to see her go. I could use all the emotional support I can get. Girl power and all that.

"I'm sorry," says Leif. "I didn't mean to embarrass you."

I settle into the chair, placing the scotch on my lap. "Yes you did."

The big guy on the table, the customer, just snorts.

"Help me out here, Art. You've been married for roughly forever," says Leif. "What do I do?"

"When in doubt, apologize. Profusely."

"Wise words," says the other dude. "I'm Ed, Leif's brother."

"Anna. Hello."

He gives me a chin tip. Now that I know they're brothers, it's obvious. Like Leif, he's a very handsome man. The same amber eyes and dark blond hair. A heavily tattooed body that's muscular, long, and lean. Must be some great genetics going on in that family. Unlike Leif, however, Ed is wearing a wedding ring. I try not to worry about what he must think of me. But he can't be happy about a married woman causing trouble for his brother. No one would willingly welcome this nonsense into their life.

It took me a week since my birthday to work up the nerve to see Leif again. Sad but true. But kicking off the divorce proceedings made it a busy week.

"How have you been?" asks Leif, eschewing further apologies.

"Good," I say, my smile weak. "You?"

He just nods. Conversation is so not flowing. The tattoo gun buzzes to life and he starts in on the piece in progress. There's a lot more blood than I imagined. But every so often Leif wipes the skin clean, and his work suddenly comes into view. The design is an old-style compass, beautiful and ornate. Above the northern point is a woman's name, 'Glenda.' I wonder if that's his wife of forever. I hope so.

"You haven't told her she looks pretty," says Art, the relationship specialist.

Leif takes in my flowy white blouse and faded blue ankle jeans with a pair of flat black leather mules. Nice but not fancy. It only took me three hours to settle on it. Why it mattered so much I'd rather not say. Friends is great and friends is fine. Thinking of anything more would be foolish. No matter how attracted I might be to the man.

"She always looks good," he says.

Nice to hear, but I'm still not sure whether I'm welcome. Or what to do. Showing up at his job might be just as great an idea as turning up at his home. What was I thinking? I could just hand over the bottle, apologize, and leave. He and I don't need to be spending time together. It was my initial plan, but now words are a tangle on my tongue. Or maybe I'm looking for excuses to stay.

"I should be finished in about ten minutes," says Leif, giving me a gentle smile. "We could try giving the whole eating-a-meal-together thing another try?"

I relax back against the seat. "Sure. That would be great."

"Better," grunts Art. "There's hope for you yet."

The weird thing about being down and out for seven months is how the world moves on without you. Great-Aunt Susan died of breast cancer. Angie and Erin finally had IVF success. A childhood hero of mine died in a drowning accident. My cousin Jack got married. A new president was elected. So many things, big and small. Then there are the movies and songs that come on TV or the radio that everyone knows except me. Little holes in my reality to remind me I was missing for a while.

"Taylor Swift put out a new album?" I ask, listening to the new tune that started playing.

Leif shoots me a grin. "Should have known you were a Swifty."

"Leave Tay Tay alone," Ed joins in with a smirk. And to think Leif called me judgmental.

"She's a fine musician and songwriter," says Art, my new hero.

"Of course she is. And yes, Anna, she did. Two albums, in fact." Leif again wipes away the blood rising to the surface on the tattoo. "About eight or nine months back."

I nod.

"Who's talking smack about Taylor?" asks Tessa, striding back into the room.

"No one," says Ed, face suddenly serious.

"We wouldn't dare," adds Leif. What a clown.

Nina Simone comes on next and Tessa hums along, swinging her hips to the music. She's wearing a pair of yellow loafers I'd kill to own. Along with a matching '50s-style tight sweater and artfully ripped jeans. I dream of being this cool. Of wearing bright colors and daring to stand out.

"I fired the new receptionist," says Tessa, apropos of nothing. "Thinking we were friends, he confided in me that he was just too hung over to join us today."

Ed shakes his head. "Fuck's sake. Why is this so hard?"

Leif's brow wrinkles into the most serious of frowns. Tessa gives his shoulder a squeeze in passing and whispers, "Not your fault. Let it go."

Curious.

"We'll find someone eventually," Tessa says in a louder tone.

Art's session finishes with smiles and manly back slapping, then Leif cleans up his area. This is more involved than I'd imagined. But then they are dealing with blood and ink and other fluids.

"Do you mind a short walk?" he asks as we head out into the afternoon sun. "Otherwise I can call a car?"

"No," I say. "A walk would be nice if we can take it slow."

Despite the long legs, he sets a pace I can manage just fine. Side by side, in perfect sync, we wander along, me hanging onto my purse strap and scotch. Him with his hands stuffed into the pockets of his leather jacket. The breeze is cool, but the sun is warm. Behind the cover of my sunglasses, I can pretty much watch him to my heart's content. Catalogue the multitude of ways in which he's different from Ryan. Which is something I probably shouldn't do, but here we are.

While my ex strides through the world toward his destination with great purpose, Leif is content to amble and take everything in. The sky, the buildings and trees, the people wandering by. He even smiles and raises a hand in greeting to some. The walk itself is an event for him, a moment to be cherished. He is a happy, open sort of person. Or at least, he gives off that impression.

While Ryan stood tall, proud, and upright, taking up as much room as possible, Leif slouches in an oddly graceful manner. Ryan reveled in being busy; our life was always planned to the nth. Work dinners, get-togethers, family outings, and so on. Something always seemed to be happening. Maybe it's why my new life is so jarring. The silence between medical appointments. The emptiness of my calendar. I need to get a life. A new one.

"Got much going on this afternoon?" I ask, making conversation.

"No. Had a cancellation." He shrugs. "Figured I'd chill."

So they're basically complete opposites. Day and night, sun and moon, et cetera.

"Care to chill with me?" he asks with a smile.

"Sure. That'd be great."

A nod. "Cool."

Ryan hated last-minute plans or alterations, while Leif seems content to live life on the fly. It's official, the two men couldn't be more different. Also, I need to stop comparing them.

"You're frowning," says Leif. "Why is that?"

I scrunch up my face. "Oh. Ah . . ."

"Be honest," he chides.

"I was thinking deep thoughts about my soon-to-be ex-husband's character."

He scratches his stubble. "Yeah, see, this is difficult for me. Because I kind of want to high-five you for dumping the asshole. And make no mistake, he is an asshole and completely undeserving of you. But on the other hand, you had your heart stomped on by that whole situation and I don't want to be an insensitive dick."

I frown. "Yeah."

He bops his head like he's listening to music. Or just agreeing with himself. "You seem like a smart woman who's got it together. So I'm sure he wasn't always a complete cock splash. At least, I hope not."

"No, he wasn't."

"But it sounds like it's probably time now to catapult that marriage into the sun."

"This is true." I heavy sigh. "You know, I used to think we were perfect. It's kind of been a wake-up call to find out that we were far from it."

He doesn't say anything. Just cocks his head to let me know he's listening.

"We used to coordinate outfits and finish each other's sentences and all that annoying couple stuff."

A grunt.

"Now I just wonder if our wardrobes were boring, if we never had an original thought between us, and perhaps urgently needed to each get a life irrespective of the other," I say. "I used to think his shortcomings were so cute. The way he'd carry on and on about work stuff. How he'd scream at the television during football games. Guess everyone's cute and funny until they're not."

"The veil has been lifted."

"Indeed."

"Relationships." His broad shoulders deflate. "What can you do?"

"I take it they're not your thing?"

He sighs. "That's a conversation that needs to be accompanied by alcohol."

"Got it."

"Listen, I'm sorry I didn't make it to your birthday bash," he says, face tense. "I, um . . . I'm not much into group things at the moment. But I hope it was a good day and everything."

"Sure. Thanks." That Mom invited him is news to me. Though she knew I'd been to see him, so I guess her inviting him makes sense. Why he's against group events, I have no idea. But it's not like they're my thing right now either. People en masse are a problem. Their opinions and expectations and just how generally overwhelming it can all be.

We wander through downtown, the city bustling around us. It's nice to be out amongst it all. I'm grateful for so many things these days. Maybe that's the main difference between old me and new me. New me knows what it's like to lose your independence. New me has been through some shit.

A few blocks away from the water we turn into a brightly painted bar in an old building. The booths have scarred old wooden tables and teal leather bench seats. It's cool. Behind the bar, a tattooed woman with a braid of gray hair hollers hello to Leif and he blows her a kiss. Obviously he's a regular. We grab a booth near the back.

"What do you suggest?" I ask, checking out the menu.

Head cocked, he asks, "May I be so bold as to order for both of us?"

"Go ahead."

"Any allergies or strong dislikes?"

"I don't like pickles."

"You don't like pickles? Weirdo." He turns in his seat, waving a hand at a passing waiter. "Two of my regular, please, Andi. And may I say you're looking particularly radiant today."

The lady smiles. "Why thank you, Leif."

"What do you have on your burger if you don't have pickles?" Leif asks, making himself comfortable. Which apparently means reorganizing the salt and pepper shakers, straightening the cutlery, and smoothing down the white paper napkin. The man is a fiddler.

"Meat, cheese, ketchup," I say. "The normal things."

"But pickles are a normal thing."

I wrinkle my nose. "Pickles are a normal thing to take off hamburgers, not put on them."

"Huh."

"What are your allergies and strong dislikes?"

"Mint," he says. "I hate that shit."

"You don't eat Mint Oreos? That's so sad. How about mint chip ice cream?"

"Yuck."

"What are you even doing with your life, Leif?"

"Living it happily mint free, is what I'm doing."

"We both hate green food items," I say. "Interesting."

"It's like we were always meant to be together." He gives me a wink to show he's joking. "What's your stance on Kermit the Frog, though?"

"He seems like a cool dude. I mean, he plays the banjo. That's pretty great."

"It is indeed. So it's not the color green, just certain food-stuffs. Okay. I can live with that," he says. "How are you taking to the single life?"

"I haven't been single in so long." My shoulders slump. "Oh, God, I'm going to have to register for a dating app. I'm actually going to have to go out and meet new people. That's so depressing and scary."

"No," he drawls. "To the contrary. It's an exciting new adventure in the life of Anna."

"Are you saying that to try and make me feel better or just pointing out my general negativity and shitty attitude?"

He grins.

Two ridiculously large and ornate beverages are placed in from of us. I'd guesstimate them to be about a quarter of a gallon of Bloody Mary cocktail topped off with an entire and intact lobster roll balancing on top of the glass.

I stare in wonder. Or horror.

"Aren't they magnificent?" asks Leif, clearly in awe of our lunch.

"This is your usual?"

"Every Saturday without fail. It's how I celebrate the upcoming weekend since I get Sunday and Monday off." His smile is beatific, there is no other word. The man is clearly experiencing his version of nirvana in this battered old booth. "Normally I'm here on my own. Sometimes Ed joins in. His wife Clem now and then too. But she just has the fried oyster bun and a beer, the coward."

"How do I even . . . what do I do with this?"

Leif laughs. He does that a lot.

Andi returns with a couple of plates and, thank God, the dismantling process can begin. I carefully remove the skewers holding the lobster roll in place and put it on a plate. The wedge of lemon comes down too. I stir up the mixture with the celery stick and skewered olives. Never has a beverage been garnished to such a degree. Now I can actually reach the edge of the glass to take a gulp. And promptly cough a lung up. That's a lot of vodka. No small amount of cracked pepper in there either.

"Too much Tabasco sauce?" asks Leif, reaching to pat me gently on the back.

"Is that what's in it?"

"You never had a Bloody Mary before?"

"No."

He puts a hand to his heart. "Aw. I'm proud to be bringing you this new and wonderful experience."

"This is hands down the strangest lunch I've ever eaten. Drunk. Whatever."

"Well, you have seven months of living to make up for," he says. "And I am here to help."

I honestly don't know when the last time I laughed was. But I'm laughing now. "You said the conversation regarding you and relationships required alcohol. Seems we've met that requirement. Go for it."

The smile swiftly disappears from his face. "I dated the woman who tried to kill my sister-in-law."

I have nothing.

"She was the receptionist at the tattoo shop. Obsessed with Ed. So she tried to kill Clem to get her out of the way. Tried twice, actually. The first time she hit her over the head with a bottle and gave her amnesia. The second time she stabbed her. Clem's lucky to be alive." His fingers beat out a frantic beat against the table. "I was staying with them and she . . . ah . . . she used me to get close to them."

Oh no. "Leif."

"This was about a year ago," he reports, matter-of-factly. "Live and learn, huh?"

I cover his hand with mine. I'm not really a touchy-feely person, but this is important.

"Yeah. So I have terrible taste in women. It's why I don't date anymore."

"Hey," I say. "You couldn't have known."

"I was sleeping with her, Anna. Of course I should have known."

"Because you're a trained psychologist with years of experience sufficient to recognize a psychopath, right?" I give his fingers a squeeze. "Leif, people like that are genius at manipulating and hiding who they are. What they are. They have to be to survive."

He slips his hand out from beneath mine, his gaze dropping to the floor.

"Does Clem blame you?" I ask.

"She's way too nice for that."

"How about your brother?"

"No."

"Just you then."

"Yes." His tone is hard. But at least he's looking at me again.

"I'm so angry that she used you and hurt you."

He grunts dismissively. As if his pain meant nothing.

"Sounds like we've both been screwed over," I say. "So let's both be sensible, rational adults and keep the blame where it belongs, on the people who did the wrong damn thing. Because anything else is pure lunacy."

His lips flatline in displeasure.

I take another sip of the Bloody Mary. "Oh God, this is like gazpacho gone wrong."

Leif gives me a look.

"If you're waiting for me to feed into your I'm-the-worst diatribe then you'll be waiting a long time."

Nothing from him.

"Is that why you tend to hang out on your own these days?" I ask. "Worried about what people will think?"

He shrugs.

It's strange. He seems like such an outgoing, friendly guy. The last person you'd expect to hide away from the world.

I carefully pick up the lobster roll and take a bite. Oh my, God. Perfection. It totally makes up for the bizarre drink and over-the-top presentation.

"You know, you look all sweet and polite, but you're actually kind of a hard-ass," he says at last.

I wipe my mouth on the napkin before speaking. "I care about my friends. That's all."

"What was your friend's name?"

"The one who slept with my soon-to-be ex-husband?"

"Yeah. That one."

"Celine."

He nods. "Celine was a moron."

My smile is slow to come, but genuine. "Thank you."

CHAPTER THREE

"**I** MISS HAVING A PERSON WHO'S ALL MINE."

Leif frowns in thought. "I miss holding hands."

I offer my hand and he takes it in his freakishly large one. His grip is warm and comforting. This is nice. Maybe I'm more of a touchy-feely person than I suspected.

"Thanks," he says.

"You're welcome."

We're sitting on his brand-new sofa. It's black linen and fits four people in an upright fashion, or two drunk people lounging and staring at nothing in general. The streetlights are on outside, night having long since fallen. Our late lunch turned into a day drinking session which morphed into evening cocktails at another local bar, followed by a visit to his condo to see his new, and only, piece of furniture.

We left the bar because I got a headache and a bit dizzy. It seems a lot of light and noise sort of does my head in after a while. Though maybe the cocktails played a role too. But sitting in his cool and quiet condo with some candles burning is just my thing.

"I miss the little everyday *I love yous*," I say.

He nods. "I miss having someone to trash-talk with. Someone safe that you can just say anything to. Really let loose and get stuff off your chest, you know?"

"Yeah." I sigh. "I keep forgetting everything that went down and for half a second I'll think, I should text Ryan. Or I should call Celine. Then I remember and it sucks."

His fingers tighten around mine and he makes a sympathetic noise in his throat. "Your turn."

"That wasn't a turn?"

"No. That was prolonged introspection on a point I'd already raised."

"Right." I try to think deep thoughts. It doesn't really work. "I miss having someone who can pick things up for me on their way home from work."

Leif rolls his head my way to give me a look of disbelief. For a big, brawny guy, he has the longest, darkest eyelashes. They almost put him on the edge of being pretty. Looking at him close up like this is distracting as all hell. No wonder my brain is having issues. If it wasn't pickled care of the blood alcohol percentage, his presence would be enough to distract me. The sheer thrill of having his attention, of being the sole subject of his focus. And now I was gushing like a schoolgirl.

"That's awful, Anna. Go again."

I groan. "God. No. I just mean . . . having someone to pick up the slack and help out, you know? Someone who's got your back. Like you're in a team. I miss having someone I can spoil and do things for too."

"Oh. Okay. Fair enough."

"It's your turn," I say. Lord knows how we even got onto this topic. What started this relationship grumble festival.

"I miss having someone I can trust."

"Agreed. I miss having someone to wake up to."

"I'm not a morning person so I'll pass on that one," he says. "No one should have to put up with me before that second cup of coffee. But I miss having someone to share meals with."

I nod. "And to have showers with. There's something so nice and intimate about that."

"I like baths."

"Baths are good."

"With like a nice-smelling oil or bubbles."

"Oh yeah." In fact, it sounds amazing. I'd invite him to have one with me, but that would probably be weird. "Definitely," I add.

He sighs. "I miss having someone to talk to last thing at night, in bed. Just to unpack the day, and life in general."

"You're not even sleeping with anyone?" I ask, beyond curious. Alcohol is so great at ridding you of pesky inhibitions. Just ask the half-empty bottle of scotch sitting on the floor, or the tabs from the bars we visited. Speaking of which, men and women were most definitely giving Leif come-hither glances, despite him being there with me. Can't really blame them, the man is so pretty. He's definitely not single from lack of options.

I may or may not have enjoyed some of the jealous glances thrown my way. My ego is running on empty these days. I'll take my wins where I can get them.

"Define 'sleeping with,'" he says.

"Sex."

"Ah." His spare hand taps out a beat against his flat

stomach. "I had a fuck buddy, but she moved away for work just before the accident."

"That's a long time to go without."

"For both of us."

"Hmm," I say. "I miss having someone who already knows what I like in bed. No need for weird or embarrassing conversations."

"Though the exploration process has its positives."

"I guess so. But in that case, why haven't you found someone new?"

"My fuck buddy was great. A good friend. I never met anyone who had an unkind word to say about her," he says. "But anytime she stayed the night, I wouldn't sleep. Couldn't."

"You didn't trust her enough to be asleep beside her?"

"I'd chosen wrong once. What if I choose wrong again?"

"No. Leif. You're not going to choose wrong." I sit up, clasping his hand in both of mine. My head might be spinning, but I am feeling all the things. My sincerity levels have got to be amped to eleven. "You need to stop being so hard on yourself. You're a really great guy and you deserve to have someone special in your life if that's what you want."

He smiles. "Thanks."

"Or a new sex friend if that's your choice."

"Thank you again. Your belief in me is appreciated and I'll give it some thought."

"You're welcome." Which gives me an idea. A really amazingly great one, actually. Quite possibly the best idea I've had in forever. Or at least today. Why it'll fix both of our problems. Neither of us needs to be lonely or be feeling generally shitty. And the whole thing about us meeting due to the accident is important. Even Leif with his fears and neurosis about choosing wrong again has to know that I'm not out to infiltrate his life for whatever dastardly reason. As far as he's concerned, I must be safe.

This will totally work.

And I can't help but stare. His bottom lip is slightly larger than his top one, making for an intriguing and potentially delicious dichotomy. A pillow-like mystery I am determined to resolve. And I bet he tastes amazing. He looks like he'd taste divine. Honest to God, I'm like a child with her nose pressed against the window of a candy store, salivating over the man.

"What are you thinking?" he asks with a quizzical amused smile. It's straight up bordering on flirty. I just know it.

Premarital eye contact. How outrageous.

The time has come to show don't tell. Besides, how would I find the words to express this genius idea? Without another thought, I lean into him and press my lips to his, hard and insistent. Adoration and horniness are the names of the game.

"Anna," he mumbles, mouth moving against mine in totally the wrong way. His breath is warm on my face and scotch scented. "What are you doing?"

"Kissing you," I mumble too. "We could both use a special sexual someone, right? Doesn't this solve both of our problems?"

Ever so gently, he pushes me back. "Not a good idea."

"No?"

"I think we're better as friends."

Oh, my God. Humiliation is mine, total and complete. "Okay."

"It's just that . . . you're going through a lot right now and I think adding me to the mix would be a mistake."

"Sure. That makes sense."

His eyes are wide with panic. "Please don't cry."

"I'm not going to cry." I sniff. "I'm just a bit embarrassed and quite possibly drunk."

He pats me awkwardly on the shoulder. "You're a very attractive woman, really."

"Great. Thanks. Let's just . . . I . . ." I trail off, because I don't know what the hell I'm doing or saying. That's the truth. What a disaster.

"Shit," he says. "This isn't working. Time to hug it out."

And before I know what's happening, I'm dragged onto his lap and caught up in a tight hold. Arms around me, Leif's face pressing into my neck, the whole thing. I'm not sure who's comforting whom here. He's arranged me to his liking and the feeling of intimacy is nice. Confusing, but nice. I haven't had anything like it in so long. The feeling of being safe and wanted and accepted. Even if he neither wants nor accepts me. Like I said, this is confusing.

"It's fine." A complete lie according to the tears flooding my face. The urge to run from this once more foreign and somewhat wild situation hits me in the gut. "Just a bit embarrassing. But yeah . . . I'm fine. I should probably go."

His hold tightens. "No."

"But—"

"You need to stop running away every time something

weird happens," he says, voice muffled, but stern. "It's interfering with our friendship."

A hand rubs circles on my back as if I were a child. It's quite soothing. This man might just make a cuddler out of me because this is good. Damn good.

"My mouth made bad choices," I sob.

"Shit happens, Anna. You just gotta let it go."

I hiccup. "O-okay."

"Deep even breaths, that's it."

"I'm sorry."

"Nothing to be sorry about," he says. "You've been through a lot lately. Get it out. All of the tears and stress and everything."

I sniffle. "Can I have some Kleenex, please?"

"Um. I only have toilet paper. Sorry."

"There's some in my purse."

"Got it," he says, depositing me back on the sofa. Then my purse is lifted off the floor and placed in my lap. Apparently Leif is a full-service-meltdown type of friend. Which is nice. I need all of the support I can get. It's nice not to cry on my own for once.

The blowing of my nose sounds like the brass section of an orchestra. But there's nothing I can do about that. I'm a soggy mess of a woman sitting on his new couch.

"It's a really nice couch," I say.

His smile is small but sweet. "You know, I bought it for you. On the off chance you ever came around again."

"Thank you. I'm so sorry I kissed you. That was a horrible, terrible mistake."

He laughs. "I wouldn't go that far."

"I didn't mean to . . . it was just, you were there and . . ."

"No problem," he says with a trademark careless grin. "I like to think we're getting all of our formative moments out of the way early. The accident, nearly getting into a fistfight with the soon-to-be ex-husband on the front lawn, you macking on me . . ."

The shame of it all. "Oh, God."

He continues to rub my back. So comforting. Right up until he opens his mouth and says, "If you want to proposition me again in a couple of months then we can revisit the topic if you're still interested."

And now he's definitely just being kind and trying to salve my pride. Thank goodness I stopped crying, at least. "It never happened and we are never discussing it again."

"Well, that's sad."

I snort. This is the most embarrassing situation. And forgetting all of my lines in the grade-four play in front of the whole damn school wasn't great. But this foolhardy performance in front of just one person is somehow far and away worse.

"Do you need more hugging?" he offers.

"No, thank you. I'm think I'm okay now."

"You know, you have an impressive amount of shit in that purse," he says, peeking into the bag on my lap.

"It's just my everyday stuff."

"Huh." He sticks his nose in a little further. "You won't believe this, but I've actually been known to leave the house without a single tube of lip balm."

"Shocking."

"It's real living-on-the-edge-type stuff, isn't it?" he asks with that amused twinkle in his eye. "Sometimes I don't even have a USB flash drive on me either."

"I used to use it for work."

"And the little notepad?"

"It's not a notepad, its blotting paper for when your face gets shiny."

"Right. That makes sense. What about the . . . is that a stain eraser pen? Holy shit, it is." His hand rifles through the contents, making itself at home. "What kind of careless bastard am I to attempt life without one of those babies on my person at all times?"

"A stained one."

He snorts. "Feel better?"

"I don't know." Only I must. Because when he smiles at me, I can't help but smile back. The man is magic.

"There we go," he says softly. Once again, Leif has made everything better. He is a great friend, loyal, kind, and true. I can only aspire to be as sweet as he is.

That my lips are still tingling doesn't matter at all. "Let's give being friends another go. I'll try not to mess it up by running away, starting a fight, or throwing myself at you this time."

He grins. "Promises, promises."

"You kissed your new male friend?"

"Yes. But it was an accident," I explain into my cell. "I was drunk and stupid."

"You were drunk?" Briar's voice rises about an octave. "You."

"I can let my hair down occasionally and enjoy myself."

"No you can't. That stick up your ass won't permit it. Or it hasn't up until now. Maybe the accident dislodged it."

"That's harsh," I grumble.

"It's the truth."

"Be nice to me, my life is spiraling."

She just laughs. I love the sound of her laughter. It's so joyous and never fails to make me smile.

"At any rate," I say. "I didn't mean to be attracted to him, so sublimating these unwanted feelings with friendship should be easy."

"Sure. Okay."

"It's not like I don't have enough other issues to deal with."

"Yep. Best of luck with that," she says. "You need to come to New York so we can visit some jazz clubs and I can experience Anna 2.0 in action."

"In case you missed it, Anna 2.0's maiden voyage didn't go so well and she's been shelved indefinitely, put in cold storage, and hidden away in a corner of the attic." I wrinkle my nose. "Also, I don't understand jazz."

"You don't need to understand it. You just need to be open to it speaking to you."

"That makes sense, I guess."

"You made out with someone who doesn't wear a suit to work. Amazing."

"Is it really, though?"

"Yes," she says, tone adamant. "This is quite the kick against your programming."

Ryan hasn't come near me since the flowers incident.

No texts or calls since the divorce papers were served. I almost miss his visits, having someone different to talk to, hearing about their everyday ordinary life. Almost, but not quite. Which just goes to show how sad my life can be. Though I definitely don't miss being reminded of his betrayal. I haven't lost my mind entirely.

I sigh. "Thank you for the divorce attorney reference. Margarita has been amazing. With no children and us both agreeing to a fifty/fifty split it should be relatively straightforward. Fingers crossed and knock on wood."

"He's accepted the inevitable, then?"

"So it would seem."

"Good."

"He's wants to keep the house."

"It's in a good school district. That might suddenly be important due to Celine expecting."

"Yeah."

"But he's made peace with the inevitable. That's a good thing."

"Pretty sure after the scene at my birthday party I've been relegated in his mind to being that crazy bitch who he's better off without," I say, doing my best not to grit my teeth. "I can't help but wonder if that was in his head all along. To drive me so fucking insane that I look like the one in the wrong. He can pat himself on the back and walk away, thinking he's rid of me."

A grunt from her. "Men. Who the hell knows?"

"Whatever works, honestly," I say. "I just want out."

She makes a humming noise.

"Bizarre to think I was going to spend my life with him and now I'll probably never speak to him again."

"Bizarre or for the best?"

"A bit of both. So how are things with you?"

"The job is fine. My apartment is terrific. And Tony wants to get back together."

"The new job is working out?"

"Yes. I like the people. And I'm on track for that corner office and partnership by forty, so yes, work is fine."

"Go, you good thing. Yay or nay on Tony?" I lie on my childhood bed, relaxing after an intense occupational therapy session this morning. Four months since waking up and there's no end to the work in sight. But I'm getting there.

"Undecided," says Briar. "He fucks like a beast, but is emotionally wanting."

"Hmm. Hard call."

"And he gave me a gift certificate for Christmas."

"That's bad?" I ask. Certificates were Ryan's gifting present of choice on account of me being impossible to shop for. I can be a fussy thing.

"It hints at a lack of careful thought and consideration when it comes to making me happy," she says.

"Okay. I can see that. Though he might just have no shopping skills."

"No." Briar sighs. "The lack of care shows up in other areas of our attempted life together as well."

"I'm sorry."

"Me too. We're compatible in some ways. Just not enough of the ones that matter." She makes a humming noise. "So I guess that answers that."

"That's sad."

"Yeah," she says. "Well, no. I'm happy to keep dating. We're not even thirty yet, for goodness sake. Who says we have to have it all together and be settled down by a certain age? That's nonsense. We're probably not even a third of the way through our lives. There's a ton more for us to explore and experience."

"That's a very valid point." I stare at the shadows on the wall made by the tree outside my childhood bedroom window. Even after months of being back it still feels strange. It feels like a failure. Like a setback. That's the truth. "Though I thought I had it all together."

"Life threw you a curve ball."

"It sure did. In the shape of a car. It knocked me on my ass." I open my eyes painfully wide. "If I haven't said it before, thank you for sticking with me through all of this and listening to my moaning."

"You're very welcome."

I don't know what else to say. My brain is both a blank and a rush of blah. Perhaps it's a mood swing kicking in, which is normal and to be expected. Another side effect to be managed.

"How did it feel kissing someone who wasn't Ryan?" she asks.

"Exciting. Weird. And then wrong. Very, very wrong. Mostly because he rejected me, which is bound to be a downer."

"Eh. It happens. Better luck next time."

"I've learned my lesson. Don't think I'll be rushing back for more anytime soon."

"Take your time. You'll be ready when it's right," she says. "And then you too can once more confront the eternal dating questions of what the fuck are they even thinking, what does it all mean, and what the hell do I do now?"

I laugh.

"Celine reached out to me again," she adds.

"Huh."

"Wanted to tell me all about the baby and so on."

I both do and do not want to know. "Okay."

Briar clears her throat. "She's had real bad morning sickness. It's been a pretty rough pregnancy, apparently. Tired and nauseous all the time."

"Oh."

"I told her I was sorry to hear that, but that unless you magically decided to forgive her I didn't have anything much to say to her."

"I appreciate the solidarity," I say. "But you don't have to pick sides. We've all been friends a long time. I understand if you want to talk to her."

"And if that had been me in that bed and my husband with Celine?"

I swallow hard. "Then I'd be done with her."

"Exactly."

"I'm sorry to hear she's having a tough time, but . . ."

"But . . ." repeats Briar.

"Exactly," I say as I nestle deeper into my old bed. The only real sign of my personality in this room is the old My Chemical Romance poster on the back of the door. I'm kind of surprised it's still there. Because otherwise, this house has always been very much my mother's domain. A pale pink feature wall and a white bedspread with small embroidered pink roses. It's a room fit for a princess. I hate pink. Mom let me redecorate when I was ten or eleven or so. Right before I hit the tween years and got myself a personality that wasn't I Love Ponies. Any attempt to update the color scheme in the past almost twenty years has been stonewalled. And as accommodating and above-and-beyond-the-call-of-duty helpful my mom has been, I need to get out of here. I need to figure out who I am now. Away from Ryan and away from the color pink. Away from the baggage of my childhood or people who think they know who I am and how I should be.

Which is what I tell Briar. "As much as I'd love to come visit you, I can't move far away yet because of all the medical appointments. But I do need my own space."

"So get your ass into gear and start looking."

"Yes." I smile. "I believe I will."

"You're really not going to let me take you, are you?" asks Mom, sitting on the edge of the sofa with her legs neatly crossed at the ankles. It's her queen pose. Very regal and self-assured. I wish I had her poise. I think I used to. But now, most of the time I feel like I'm stumbling from one disaster to the next. Leif would probably tell me to embrace the journey, or something like that. And today I am taking a step in the forward direction, which is great. Two weeks' worth of legal appointments and apartment hunting have led to this moment. To a chance of some independence from both Ryan and my parents. I am an adult, dammit. I can do this.

"I feel like I need to do this by myself," I answer.

"I still think it's too soon."

"I disagree. It'll be fine."

"If you say so."

And I mean it. It'll be fine because I have a plan. Everything I do takes a bit more effort and organization these days. A bit more time to get ready and get sorted. However, I'm up to the challenge. Hell yes I am.

My cell chimes with a text.

Leif: Talk to me.

Me: Greetings. How are you?

Leif: Talk to me as if I'm someone you actually know and like.

Me: That was me being nice. This is a trap. Whatever I say you're going to give me trouble.

Leif: Of course I am. You went silent on me again for two damn weeks.

"Is everything alright?" asks Mom.

"Ah, yes. Just a friend." I frown even harder, because what the hell do I say to him? He kind of has a point. I have a bad habit of going into hiding when things go wrong. And because I'm me and this is my life, things tend to go wrong often.

Leif: Open the door.

Me: What?

Which is when someone knocks at the door and huh. How about that? Mom smothers a brief smile, and what is going on here? The woman is neither surprised that we have a guest nor making a move to answer said door. I sense a setup. A bizarre one.

When I open it, Leif is standing there all ridiculously hot and happy with himself. Is it any wonder I did the wrong thing and kissed him? I'm not used to being around beautiful sunshine-y people. Wild men with long hair and ink who keep smiling at me and giving me chances when I mess up. They're an adventure all their own. I don't know how to act. I don't know how to be just his friend. Invasive naked thoughts keep taking over. I feel like a complete asshole for objectifying him all of the time, when I know good and well that there's so much more to him than how he looks. But here we are. Shame on me.

He waltzes right past me and says, "Hey, Denise. Nice to see you again."

"Leif." Mom gives him a polite nod and smile. "Welcome to our home."

He nods and looks around. The beige color scheme does not impress, according to his expression. Same goes for the collection of golfing trophies on the mantel. Which is where Dad is, at golf. I don't know why he doesn't just move to the course.

Leif is the last person who should be judging Mom's suburban castle. Any bet his condo is still rocking the blank-white-wall look.

Mom fetches her purse from the side table. "I have a thing at the church."

"So you didn't want to take me after all," I say.

Her smile is brief. "I knew you wouldn't let me. That's why I asked Leif."

"You and Leif talk?" I ask, tone somewhat incredulous.

"Sure," he says, leaning against the living room doorway. "Denise and I are old pals."

"Less use of the word *old*, thank you," reprimands my mother.

"Sorry." He crosses his arms. "We're house shopping, huh?"

"Looking at apartments to rent."

A nod. "Don't worry, I borrowed Clem's SUV. You won't have to try to hop on the back of my bike in your pretty dress."

It's a simple green maxi dress with a cream cardigan and matching sandals. I'd like to think it says responsible adult who pays her own bills and won't trash your property, but it probably just says I couldn't be bothered with pants. Such is life. He's wearing an old The Clash tee, black jeans, and sneakers. His hair is tied back into a man bun that my fingers itch to tousle. There it is again. The bad and wrong thoughts. All of this makes me wonder when I started feeling so distinctly unattached. So single. It's weird.

When I woke up from the coma, Ryan's was the first face I wanted to see. I know that much. But when the truth of what he'd been up to came out, followed by all of his excuses, which were then superseded by his attempts to gaslight me, things changed. Dramatically. Guess my love for him was conditional after all. Conditional upon him not treating me like shit. Though inconvenient thoughts of my new male friend does not mean that I'm ready to start dating or actually attempt a relationship with someone. The whole idea just freaks me out. I need time to grieve the end of the relationship. A chance to pull myself together and figure out where all of this leaves me.

So first up, I shall go seeking domestic independence in the form of an apartment.

"Best of luck, sweetheart," says Mom, waiting to lock the front door. She sure is in a rush. Also, she's wearing a rather dapper black pantsuit with a fancy lace camisole underneath. Curiouser and curiouser.

"You're going to a church thing?" I ask.

She nods.

"I'll see you later then."

"Yes." And she's gone. Huh.

Leif and I head toward a black Jeep waiting in the driveway. Like a gentleman, he opens the passenger-side door for me. Someone raised him right.

"How about that gleam in Denise's eye," he whispers as I climb into the vehicle. "Your mom is totally going for a hookup with your dad at some fancy hotel in town."

"What?" I do not screech. It just kind of sounds that way. Unfortunately.

"I'm just guessing. I could be wrong." He closes the door and jogs around to the other side of the vehicle. "Were you unaware that your parents still have sex?"

"No, but—"

"They're not that old, Anna. And with you in the house, I can understand why they might want to get away for a little privacy now and then."

"I know that, but—"

"Gotta admire them for it, really."

"Would you stop interrupting me and let me finish?" I ask, aggrieved.

"Sorry." He starts the engine and backs us out of the driveway. "You were saying?"

"I don't know," I say, clutching my purse and my list of

addresses. I'd probably be clutching my pearls if I actually owned any. "You've got me all flustered. Give me a minute to get my brain back on track. And stop talking about my parents having sex. It's weirding me out."

He laughs all low and dirty like. "You sweet, innocent naïve creature."

"Yes, that's exactly what I am. And I texted you the other day to ask how you were and to talk smack about pickles," I remember out of nowhere. "So there. I did not completely go into hiding."

"But when I answered, did you text me back?"

"Maybe not. I wasn't sure what to say. Then I overthought it and it all sort of went to hell so I gave up. I mean, what if I said the wrong thing. Or if whatever I said was taken the wrong way due to lack of context? Communicating with people is hard sometimes."

"Wasn't communicating with people part of your job?"

"Actually, Celine handled most of the front desk management. I was more out back concocting schemes and handling paperwork."

"Huh."

"The truth is, I'm still mildly horrified about the kiss," I admit. "And then I overthink everything and get worried that you are kind of different from the people I'm used to dealing with. Not in a bad way. To the contrary, in a very good way. But still different. I'm not always sure how you're going to react." I pause to take a breath, not blathering at all. "Not that I believe you're going to be harsh or anything. I just worry sometimes, and then I feel awkward, and then I kind of spiral."

He just blinks.

"What? My neurosis makes sense on a certain level when you think about it."

He raises a brow. "You sure about that?"

"Shut up."

"Sorry, sorry." His smile is brief. A bare hint of the usual happy. "I don't like that you worry or feel uncomfortable with me sometimes."

"It's not your fault and there isn't anything you can do about it. It's me. I just need a bit of time to adjust. Really."

"In that case, C-minus for effort," he announces. "Must try harder with the texting. I look forward to practicing with you. And I'll always give you the benefit of the doubt, I promise. I'm not going to jump to the worst conclusion over something you say, Anna."

"No. That's more my kind of thing."

He takes a deep breath. "Now that was a very beige house you grew up in. Though I found the occasional tan accent to be quite out there and daring, really."

"And you call me judgy. Hey, it was raining this week," I remember all of a sudden. "Was your arm okay?"

"Eh. Some aches and pains. Nothing out of the ordinary," he says. "Where are we going?"

"There's one in Oakdale that looked okay."

"Wrong side of the highway."

"I know, and transportation is kind of an issue for me these days," I say. "The less I need to drive, the better. There was a more promising one in the West End."

"Okay," he says, heading in that direction. "So are we going to talk about that kiss?"

I wrinkle my nose. "No."

Another laugh.

"There's nothing to say. I made that clear at the time. It never happened and we're moving on." I raise my chin in defiance. The truth is, I need to be single for a while. Sex friends are all nice and well and useful, but the focus here is on me getting my life together. Not on finding a transitional person to help me get over Ryan. Acclimatizing to being single is what's best for me right now. I don't need sex (involving other people) and I don't need my hand held. I am a grown-ass woman. "I thought about a small house, but the fact of the matter is, I have enough going on looking after myself. Taking on a yard as well seemed foolishly optimistic, even if having a little garden would be lovely."

"Not to be an asshole and suggest you're unable to cope on your own or anything, but you're okay with living on your own?"

I grip the seat as we turn around a corner. "Please slow down a little."

He darts a look at me.

"Sorry. I get panicky in cars sometimes."

"Of course," he says, easing his foot off the accelerator. "I'm sorry. Should have thought of that."

I swallow hard, doing my best to relax. Shoulders down, breathing even and all that. "Anyway . . . what are my options? Sharing a house isn't appealing and I'm fortunate that I can afford my own small space. For now, at least. My friend Briar would love me to move to New York, but I'm not so sure about that."

"New York?" he asks, brows raised and eyes surprised.

"Yeah. A clean slate might be nice, but I don't know."

"Big cities are fun to visit, but I wouldn't want to live there," he says. "Portland's great. A bit slower and smaller. Plenty of cool bars and nightlife if that's your thing. Not so small that everyone's in your business."

"Speak for yourself. Me and my drama is the talk of the 'hood."

"Yeah, well . . . you've been a bit too exciting lately." He winces. "I know what that feels like. After the truth came out about my crazy ex trying to kill Clem, it felt like everyone in the world knew. There were pictures in the papers and a police investigation and you name it. But, Anna, these things do calm down sooner or later. How's the divorce going? Is the douchebag fighting you?"

"No. I think he's given up on messing with me and is focusing on his new and improved family with Celine." Ugh. Whatever. I do not care. I refuse to care. "We're dividing up the things from our house."

"What'd you make a grab for?"

"First up was the chunky mahogany dining table and chairs with the matching sideboard."

He grins. "I knew you owned a sideboard. Bet there's even linen napkins in there."

"Shut up." I smile too. "Then I got petty and went for the big-screen TV and sound bar that he loves more than life, but is too cheap to go for straight up because he knows it's not the thing worth the most money in the house."

"Atta girl. Get him where it hurts."

"Apparently I still have some aggression issues to work through, but such is life. He went first for the Sub-Zero fridge with the glass doors that his parents got us as a wedding present," I say. "But it's too big for most apartments and houses and its resale value is not that amazing. Nor do I want anything that came from his parents, who have supported their darling boy through his screw-up one hundred percent. Not that I really expected any different."

"You're so cunning. I love it."

"Thank you. Know your enemy, right?"

"Remind me never to divorce you." He gives me a wink. Him and those damn winks. They turn my stomach upside down each and every time, dammit. "And you've obviously given this a lot of thought."

"Half of that life and its contents are mine. Because of his bad choices we have to go through all of this." I sigh. "It's hard to think about anything else right now, honestly. I may or may not have a couple of revenge fantasies running through my head. Nothing that would physically harm either one of them. Just really inconvenience the shit out of them and teach 'em a lesson, you know?"

He just nods.

"It's funny. Well, it's not funny. It's strange, maybe." I shift in the seat, all the better to see him.

"Go on."

"I could almost understand him needing physical affection or relief involving someone other than himself after so long," I say. "If he'd gone to a sex worker to get it, I think I could have accepted that better given the circumstances. I would have been hurt initially, sure. But then I would have understood, I think."

"Okay."

"Is it weird to talk about this?" I ask, feeling distinctly weird about it. "Maybe it's weird to feel this way at all."

"No. You're safe with me."

"Right. Okay." I take a deep breath. "Thank you."

"That's all?"

I shrug. "What more is there to say? He didn't go to a sex worker. He went to my best friend. And she obviously reciprocated, and that relationship continued well beyond the point he promised me. Obviously. Because if it had only happened once at her apartment with a condom, there likely wouldn't be a baby on the way."

"You asked for details?"

"I wanted to know if they'd done it in our house," I explain. "In our bed. I wanted to know if he'd protected himself and me from any possible diseases or whatever. How disrespectful and stupid the sin was, exactly."

A nod.

"The first place is on West Street."

"Tell me about it," he says.

"Two bedrooms, one bathroom, wood-burning fireplace and big bay windows."

"Sounds nice. What else have you got?"

"A new one-bedroom, one-bathroom in the East End and an old one-bedroom, two-bathroom in West Bayside."

"That's a lot of bathrooms for one person," he says.

"And both have heated floors."

"Delightful."

"The question is, do I want to go more old-fashioned or something urban loft style with high ceilings," I ponder. "I've never lived on my own before. Never gotten to choose my own place."

"I'd be more interested in location so you can walk wherever you want to go out. What restaurants and bars are nearby and so on," he says. "You're investing in a possible lifestyle, you know?"

"That makes sense."

"So you basically don't know what kind of apartment you want or where you want it, apart from roughly somewhere in the city."

"Basically."

"Any concerns about living on your own so soon after everything?" he asks, shooting me a glance. "Again, not to take the wind out of your sails, young Anna. Just wondering."

"Yes," I admit. "Some. But as much as I love my parents, I can't keep living with them. For all of our sakes."

"Fair enough. What about work?"

"Hoping to find something part-time in a couple of months maybe. It depends how rehab goes. I think I could handle maybe fifteen hours a week to start off. That's what I'm working toward, at least."

"What about money? Not to be nosey, but how is the divorce affecting things?"

"It would probably be more sensible to wait until everything is sorted, but due to Ryan buying me out of my half of the house I can afford something small."

He hits the signal and pulls over beside a park. Children are playing on the slides, all happy and carefree. Big old trees shade the playground. It's picturesque. There's a small pain inside of me at the sight of the children. Not the greater hurt that I'd have imagined the scene would cause. Maybe I wasn't completely ready for being a parent. Or maybe the idea of bringing a child into the world while everything is so unsettled just doesn't appeal. I don't know. But there's time to figure it out later with the right person, which Ryan obviously isn't. What I thought was a bright and brilliant future with him is most definitely not and I need to get used to that idea. Embrace it. I need to open myself to the new challenges or something.

"Okay," says Leif. "Crazy idea time."

"Crazy idea time?"

"Move in with me."

"What?" And there I go sounding screechy again. So uncool.

He nods, all self-assured. Not an iota of doubt in his amber gaze. "Firstly, you have furniture, right?"

"Some. Yes. But—"

"Secondly," he says, then stops. "Oh, shit. I interrupted you again. Sorry. You go."

"What is secondly?" I ask, crossing my arms.

"It wouldn't be some weird roommate situation with me. We could help each other. I'll be around in case you need a hand. You'd have your space without being totally on your own. Just in case . . ."

"And?"

"And you'll be there in case I, um . . . like if I need a jar opened or something. The strain on my arm can be quite painful." He grimaces as if to display this unfortunate weakness. The clown. Like he isn't muscled to perfection.

"You're such a male," I say. "I'll pretend I believe you."

"I can even tell you if you need to pack an umbrella each day. Very useful to have around."

"What else?"

"You don't exactly know what you're doing or where you really want to be just yet. Therefore, committing to a lease doesn't make sense." He smiles all confident. "You wouldn't have to do that if you moved into my spacious and light-filled spare bedroom. Do what you want. Come and go as you please."

"This is all about helping me. You're putting yourself out for my benefit."

"No. Not entirely. I could definitely use some help paying for the place, okay?" He sags against the headrest. "Truth is, I haven't been able to work as much in the last while due to the accident. It's going to take me some time to catch up. Whether you stay for a week or a year, it's going to help me moneywise."

"I don't know."

"I've been thinking about getting a roommate. Honestly. So this would be perfect. It could be like your soft launch."

It's a lot to think about.

"Just say yes."

"Don't push me. I'm considering things," I say. "What about the unfortunate kissing incident?"

"What unfortunate kissing incident?"

"Good answer." I smile. "How about the fact that we're fundamentally opposites?"

He blinks. "Please explain."

"I'm hospital corners and you're free and easy."

"Ah. Gotcha." He scratches at the stubble on his jaw. "Well, I figure that means we'll complement each other and enlarge our experience of the world and people and stuff."

"And stuff?"

"Yeah. C'mon, Anna. You're clean, unlikely to host loud parties or annoy the living shit out of me. We get along fine. You pay attention to things I tend to forget about. Like furniture," he says. And he's not wrong. "This is a win-win situation for both of us."

"Oh, God. I don't know."

"If it doesn't work out you leave. Easy as that." He taps his fingers against the steering wheel. "Anna, baby. C'mon."

Here's the thing about how my life has gone so far . . . playing it safe, being cautious, hasn't gotten me far. I'm living back at home with my parents, for goodness sake. The man who made the most sense to me let me down in the worst way imaginable. One of the women I used to confide just about everything to stabbed me in the back. Safe, cautious, sensible—these things have not worked out. Maybe it's time I try a new approach.

"Ugh. Okay. Yes." And it was not his use of the term *baby* that won me over. It was something else.

He claps his hands in delight like a child. "Excellent."

"We give it a try for a few weeks and see how things go," I say. And who knows, it might work out. Because I can't have a crush on my roommate. That would just be stupid. A rookie mistake. Things are complicated enough as it is. I'll get over my unfortunate and weird feelings for Leif. Therapy and getting divorced are sure to keep me busy. Grieving the end of my marriage and getting used to life without Ryan. Stuff like that. Life sure comes at you fast. "See if it works and if we're both comfortable with the arrangement and so on."

"Whatever you say." He grins. "This is going to be great."

CHAPTER FOUR

"I THINK I LIKED IT BETTER BACK OVER THERE," ED'S WIFE, Clem, says.

Ed gives her a pained look. Fair enough. He and Leif have been moving things around all day. Which can't be good for Leif's arm, but he refuses to take it easy.

"The light is just so nice there," she continues arguing her case.

"I think they're running out of oomph for the day," I say. "Might be time to break out the beers and leave the rest for later."

She sighs wistfully. Her commitment to the placement of my side table is immense. "You may have a point."

I'm just pleased to have a new home that is not my parents'. After a busy two weeks, I am indeed now moved in with Leif. My new roommate and friend. Nothing more. Not that it needed to be said because it's already obvious.

Two weeks was also a necessary period to get the furniture out of the old house, et cetera. It's nice to be surrounded by my own stuff again. I'd had concerns it would be strange, since it came from my life with Ryan. But nothing feels especially off. New and different, but not off. Though I ordered a new bed.

No way did I want anything to do with the mattress from my past. That thing is cursed for all time.

Clem hands out beers, earning a kiss on the cheek from her doting husband. She was attacked a bit over a year ago, and lost all of her memories, though she was only briefly in a coma.

Clem and Ed live in the condo beside ours, along with their dog Gordy, who is asleep under the dining table. He's a silver Staffordshire terrier and a very good boy. Apparently some creeper dude by the name of Tim used to live in this condo, so everyone was pleased as punch when he left and Leif got the place. They're obviously all close. A loving family. It's nice to see them interacting and to be around new people. Today feels like a big step forward. No more stagnating. I am rebuilding my life from the ground up.

"So that's what the place looks like with stuff in it. I like it." Hand on hips, Leif looks around with a pleased grin. "What do you think, Anna?"

I smile. "I think it's all good."

"Excellent."

"It's like a real home now," says Clem. "You hadn't made much of an effort with it, Leif. I guess you're the type that needs a woman to step in and sort things out."

Ed hides a smile.

"Thanks for the feedback, Clem." Leif salutes her with his bottle of beer.

"You're welcome." The woman can be blunt, but I like it. Fuck faux politeness.

Why do we do that? Why do we hide our thoughts and feelings from people? If we can't trust who we're talking to, then do we really even need them in our lives? Though if we're likely to hurt someone with a possibly unnecessary comment, then I guess I can see the point. Or if they're just an acquaintance, but someone who for one reason or another we need in our lives . . .

Huh. People are tricky. Relationships are hard.

Perhaps we'll never really know what most of those around us are really thinking. Maybe that's for the best. I don't know. All my deep thoughts have given me is a renewed sense of confusion.

"I don't think we should run away together after all," Leif says to Clem with a teasing smile. "Let's stay with my fool of a brother and make him move furniture around for the rest of his days. It'll irritate him no end, my lovely Clementine."

"One of these days when you're flirting with her I'm going to hit you with something," says Ed with a pained expression. "Like my fist."

Leif just blinks. "So violent."

"Your mom said you two used to fight constantly when you were kids," says Clem. "I think I prefer you both having grown out of that stage."

"Seconded," I add.

"What are you thinking about?" asks Leif, joining me at the table. "What does that look on your face mean?"

My stomach grumbles. Talk about rude. "It means I need food."

"In the mood for Mexican?"

"Always," I say, pulling my cell out of my back jean pocket. "I'll get it. To thank everyone for helping with the move. You guys will stay for dinner, right?"

"We'd love to," says Clem.

"Great." I ask for recommendations, and we settle on a local place with good reviews and get busy ordering a bit of everything. "Can't believe you didn't even own silverware or plates."

Leif just shrugs. "I stole a mug from work. That's all I really needed. Delivery places give you those bamboo cutlery sets all of the time. Seemed a shame to waste them."

"Very environmentally conscious of you."

"Nuh." Ed snorts. "He's just lazy and he hates shopping. If Mom knew he'd been using empty peanut butter jars as drinking glasses she'd have been over here getting his ass organized months ago."

"You know, I think I prefer environmentally conscious," confides Leif. "Makes me sound good."

His brother just shakes his head.

"He's right about Mom, though. I am her baby and proud."

"I can tell you're the youngest of the family," I say. "That makes sense."

"Because of my youthful good looks?"

"Sure." I smile. "That's exactly it."

Clem laughs.

She and Ed have been married for about a year and are still firmly in the honeymoon period. It's obvious in the way they're always touching and looking at each other. They're so in sync.

Ryan and I used to be that way. Before the accident happened, we were in a good place. We didn't fight a whole lot because often it just wasn't worth the drama. He could sulk for sustained periods, which was tiresome. I picked my battles. The things that were really worthwhile, that I was willing to dig in over and make my point be heard. I'm not sure if that's healthy or not, censoring yourself in that way.

Love is such a strange thing. The whole idea of making a

commitment to someone. There's no guaranteed return, just the chance to give. And we throw our heart and soul into the situation, hoping for the best. It's a giant leap of faith. Nice to see it can work out for some people. I don't want to get jaded and bitter, but now and then it's definitely tempting. In the far distant future I'll meet someone who'll be so far superior to Ryan and his hazy loyalties and wandering cock that my first marriage and its demise will all seem like a bad dream. One day. No rush.

"You're an only child," says Leif. "You can't speak."

"True. I was a late-in-life surprise. My parents didn't really mean to have kids."

"No?"

"No," I say. And I don't have anything to add to that. That information about my folks was kind of an overshare, actually. The sort of thing I'd normally only talk about with Briar and Celine. But something about Leif makes me a little too comfortable. Too trusting. Or maybe I just shouldn't be so paranoid in the first place. Who knows?

"Well, I'm glad that they did." Leif gives me a smile. He always knows what to say to make everything better.

"So are we," says Clem.

It's nice to make new friends.

"And when you're ready to date again, I know this great guy," she continues. "He works in a coffee shop across from the bookstore. Just a really pleasant person, you know?"

"Oh," I say.

Leif makes a derisive-type noise in his throat. "I think Anna can do better than just a really pleasant person, don't you?"

Clem frowns, obviously thinking it over. "It didn't sound like such a bad idea until I said it out loud. He's very nice."

"Boo," says Leif. "Nice and pleasant."

"You think he'd be a dud in the sack?" asks Clem.

"Bound to be."

"You could always set her up with Rahul," suggests Ed. "He owns a tattoo parlor in town. Good guy. I have no idea nor do I want to know what he's like in bed, however."

"Not Rahul." Leif crosses his arms over his chest. "Tattoos aren't really her thing."

"I don't have anything against tattoos," I say, my gaze narrowed.

"Yeah, but you're more traditional in your tastes generally. And there's nothing wrong with that."

My chin goes up. "And yet I'm pretty sure it wasn't a compliment."

"Just stating a fact, Anna. I'm not trying to hurt your feelings or anything."

Ed and Clem watch us, heads turning this way and that as if it were a tennis tournament.

"Yeah, but you kind of have anyway. Guess I'm sensitive when it comes to this sort of thing," I say, settling into the argument. Discussion. Whatever.

Leif's mouth opens, but nothing comes out.

"Since the way I approached life didn't wind up working out for me so well, maybe altering my view of things or previous tastes is a good idea."

"Maybe it is."

"I could date someone outside of my immediate experience without the world ending. Someone with tattoos might be fun."

"If you wanted to," he says, sounding a bit tense. "Sure."

"It might even be good for me to try new things."

A nod. "Yeah. I just didn't . . ."

"You just didn't what?" I prod.

His gaze slides over me, assessing. Lines furrow his forehead and his lips are thin. "I'm not trying to cage you in, Anna. Do what you like. I was just looking out for you is all."

Clem and Ed share a look. No idea what it means.

A small smile lights Leif's face as he steps closer. "That felt weird. Hug it out with me."

"It was just a small disagreement."

His arms open, enveloping me in heaven. There's no other word for it as he rocks me gently from side to side. "You're right and I'm wrong. There. Done."

I wrap my arms around his waist. How can I resist?

"You're very cuddly," he says. "This is nice."

"It is."

"Now that we live together, we can do this all the time. Isn't that great?" he asks.

"Very."

Clem makes a noise in her throat.

Leif turns his head. "What?"

"Nothing," she says with a smile in her voice. "Nothing at all."

And she's got a point. I step back, covering my chest by crossing my arms for various secret reasons. Fine. Because of hard nipples. Ye Lords, the embarrassment. Leif is a consummate flirt. I've already seen it many times. It doesn't mean anything when he acts sweet and I'd be a fool to lose touch with that fact. A fool with a hopeless crush on her roommate. A silly individual whose lady parts need to cease and desist. Surely I know better than that?

I do not know better than that. This is made clear in no time at all.

It's about one in the morning on my first night of sharing the condo. I don't know what woke me. A disturbance in the force, maybe. Either that or some small noise caused by Leif doing push-ups on the living room floor like his life depends on it. That he's doing them in only a pair of gray sweatpants is something I'm just going to ignore. The way they adhere to his butt is a thing of beauty, though. How the dim lighting and sheen of sweat on his bare back accentuates the long, lean slabs of muscle and dips of his spine. This really is something.

Being sexually aware of other men in my life is no big deal now (mostly). The rush of guilt and longing to hide it all away is fading. Since I'm no longer attached to Ryan, save for some paperwork that's in the process of being filed, I'm making my peace with the situation. I'm done with any and all forms of suffering due to my ex's bad choices. Feelings and hormones and all of those things can come back on line. Weird how it only seems to happen around my new roommate, though.

"Hey."

"Hey." He pauses, sucking in a deep breath. The muscles in his arms tremble with strain. "Sorry. Did I wake you?"

"No." I don't actually know what woke me, so it's not exactly a lie. "Can't you sleep?"

"Nightmare." His voice is clipped. All ease, he climbs to his feet and heads into the kitchen for a glass of water. His hair is tied back from his face, his cheekbones stark. There's something raw and real about him. Like with the flirtatious behavior and his usual joie de vivre stripped away, the bare bones of the man are exposed. "Want a drink?"

"I'm fine, thanks. Was it about the accident?"

A nod.

"So you wear yourself out physically to get back to sleep?"

One shoulder lifts a little. It's a half shrug. As much as he can manage, apparently. And it's the arm that wasn't injured in the accident, so lord only knows how bad the other is hurting. "The idea is to keep pushing until exhaustion and lactic acid burn crowd out everything else. Sometimes it works."

"Do you want to talk about it?" I don't think he does, given his body language, but it seems only polite to ask.

A brief shake of the head as expected.

"Okay." And I just stand there in the living room doorway not sure what to do. The overexertion can't be good for his arm, but I'm neither his mother nor his keeper. I know what it's like to have people getting in my face about issues relating to the accident, so I'm not about to do the same to him. Though it's tempting.

Worrying about him also means that my mind is now wide the fuck awake and going at about a billion miles an hour. Poor Leif. Poor hot, half-naked Leif. It basically just goes on and on like that. Sex thoughts inundating my mind. All of the inappropriate in all of the land is mine.

Since I won't be sleeping anytime soon, I figure I might as well do something constructive with the time. Also, there's the happiness I'm feeling, yet again, that I'm in a space that's fifty percent my own. Within reason, I can do whatever the heck I like without Mom butting in and asking what I'm doing, and getting anxious about me using her things and making a mess in her perfect house. Getting a glass of water was enough to make her run for the kitchen to check on things. I come by my neurosis honestly.

"I think I might bake something," I say.

"You're going to bake?" He tilts his head. "Now?"

"Yeah."

"Huh. What are you thinking of making?" He leans against the kitchen counter, arms crossed over his still very much bare chest. Leif has a little more chest hair than Ryan. I don't think I ever had strong opinions on chest hair before, but let's take a moment here and get introspective. There's not a '70s porn star excessive amount of chest hair going on, just enough to make things interesting. Enough to make me want to stroke my fingers over his pecs and flat nipples. To curl my fingers around his firm biceps and lean in for a sniff.

Is it wrong to want to smell your roommate? It is. I know it is.

I'm objectifying him again, dammit. I am the actual worst. Leif is just a friend. That's all he wants and I'm going to respect his decision, if it's the last thing I do. This may involve me donning a chastity belt, or something, but such is life. My hormones will have to calm the fuck down. Because having him for a friend is pretty damn awesome all on its own. Think I might have to pluck my eyes out to stop with the staring, though. Nothing less will do. Me and my surprisingly dirty one-track mind are an issue.

"Um . . ."

He waits.

Right, baking. We were talking about baking.

"Well, what have we got?" I head over to check out the pantry and fridge. Given Leif keeps scotch, beer, ketchup, and not much else, I'd brought groceries with me. Just the basics. Enough to get started. "No bananas, so we can't make banana bread. No blueberries, so we can't make pie or muffins. I know, how about brownies?"

"Brownies would be amazing."

"Okay. Done."

"It's weird having someone in this space," he says.

"Weird bad or weird good?"

"The latter."

I smile.

First, we both wash our hands. Next, out come the butter and eggs from the fridge. Then the flour, sugar, baking powder, and cocoa from the pantry. Excellent. We've got everything we need for a chocolate fix in the wee hours of the morning while sleep has left us high and dry. Though maybe not dry in my case, because he still hasn't put a shirt on and he is right there and his sweat is apparently a beckoning call to my overactive hormones and lady parts.

Meanwhile, Leif starts rifling through cabinets, searching for something. "I'm sure I had a bowl somewhere. Not sure about a big spoon."

"I didn't see any while I was unpacking. My mixing bowl is in the bottom right cabinet."

I tie on my apron. "Could you please preheat the oven to 350 degrees?"

"On it." He does as told, casting me a curious look over his shoulder. "Anna, does everything you own match?"

"No. Not everything. Though I do kind of stick to a color scheme. And I like things to look a certain way." Oh dear. It's a little odd seeing my French navy-and-white-colored cooking set in a new space. But since Leif only owns a bed and one cool black linen sofa, everything basically coordinates. I'd cope if it didn't. But my obsessive-compulsive tendencies, inherited thanks to Mom, are happy. "So the real answer there I guess is maybe a yes?"

"Right," he says. "Are you going to freak out if I'm being messy and leave something lying around?"

"That depends. What sort of something?"

"I don't know . . ."

"You probably should have thought of this issue before inviting me to move in, by the way."

He sighs. "What if my laptop is lying around?"

I shrug. Care factor nil.

"Okay." He taps a finger against his lips in thought. "How about an item of dirty laundry?"

"I'd probably just throw it back in your room so I don't have to look at it."

He contemplates this answer. "Fair enough. I think the cushions and throw you put on the couch are nice."

"Great!" I smile. "You know, I'm not as anal as I used to be. But I do like things the way I like them. I'm going to survive if they're not perfect, however."

"Perfect is hard."

"Perfect is impossible and unattainable," I correct him with a smile. "Life isn't perfect, Leif. Neither of us are perfect either. Nor do I expect us to be. It's hard enough just figuring out who you are and being yourself in this world. Why heap on the expectations and make the whole thing that much harder for yourself and everyone around you?"

"Good point."

"Thank you. I've got a bit more perspective these days. Having your life upended gives you a certain kind of wisdom, apparently."

"Well, I for one no longer live in fear of clashing with your color scheme," he says.

"Excellent."

"I did, however, expect something more like silk for your nightwear." His amber gaze runs over me from top to toe. It's quite thrilling. He's never really shown anything beyond a casual interest in my appearance before. "Something . . . flowy," he says. "You know?"

"Something flowy?" I look over my pale blue men's pajamas. "These are flowy."

"No, they're baggy. There's a difference."

"Yes. Well. They're comfortable. Thanks for the feedback, and I'm sorry I let you down on the risqué lingerie front."

"That's okay," he says, all magnanimous like. The idiot.

But if he was having horny thoughts about what I wear to bed then I don't feel quite so bad about my continued and ongoing objectification of the man. So there.

While I never asked Leif if he wanted to bake with me, we just kind of fall into sync in the small kitchen. His energy is back. His happy vibe. Guess distraction can work wonders for dark moods and thoughts. Same goes for the promise of chocolate and sugar. While he doesn't seem to have much experience, he is eager to learn. Something I heartily approve of. Mom liked the idea of me learning to cook, just not the actual me-being-in-her-kitchen part of things. Mostly my grandma taught me. She didn't get as cranky if I dropped flour on the floor. She used to make the best Mexican wedding cakes I ever tasted.

"What next?" he asks.

"Would you mind greasing the pan while I melt the butter?"

"Sure." First he picks up his cell, putting on some music. An old Nina Simone song about feeling good. Perfect for kitchen shenanigans at odd hours of the morning. While I'm a great believer in kitchen safety, a bit of hip swaying in time to the beat never hurt anybody. Probably. I'm not actually much of a dancer. It requires a level of coordination I never quite managed to achieve. Nor was I blessed with a decent singing voice. But I do love music. The way it sweeps you up and fills you with emotions. The way it tells a story and takes you on a journey. The art of it all.

Which is when I realize my heart is light. Being here, doing this with him, feels right. That's nice. It's good. I choose to take it as a sign that I'm clearly on the right life track.

"It's always about you," he says out of nowhere, voice subdued and dark gaze fixed on the pan. "The nightmares, or flashbacks. I'm not sure what they are, but they come at night. You being stuck in the car and me not able to get you out in time before something worse happens. Like it catches on fire or a tree limb crushes it or another vehicle slams into you and . . . there's not a fucking thing I can do. I just watch you die over and over again in all these fucked up violent ways and I hate it. I hate that I let you down."

My fingers tighten around the wooden spoon.

"Hope I'm not freaking you out," he says in a gruff voice.

"No. It's okay. I asked."

"Yeah, but . . . shit."

"It's okay, Leif. Tell me."

And he does. He opens his mouth and lets it all out. "I'm

always standing there with my stupid arm all messed up and blood leaking out of me and the pain just about bringing me to my knees. And you're stuck. You're trapped. And I'm fucking helpless. There's nothing I can do and no one will stop and help. Cars keep right on streaming past. No one giving a fuck. And I just want to scream."

I lick my suddenly dry lips. "That's awful."

"Yeah."

"It wasn't your fault, Leif. You did all you could do," I say. "Mom told me, they had to cut me out of my car. There was no way you could have—"

"I know."

I take a deep breath. "Your subconscious just needs to get the message."

"Yeah."

"I'm sorry."

He just looks at me. "Anna, it wasn't your fault either. That car lost control and swerved into your lane. There was nowhere you could go. Nothing you could do."

"I don't like that you're still hurting."

"Yeah, well . . . a few night terrors won't be the end of me." He turns away. "And here you are, safe and well and all in one piece. Life is good. Most of it."

I don't know what to say.

On one hand, it sucks not being able to remember the accident. Not being able to dissect it inside my skull and know for certain that I did the best I could. No one has really been able to give me the right answer about that day. The one that will set my mind at ease. But on the other hand, if I did remember, I'd probably be having nightmares about it, along with the weird ones I don't tend to talk about. Because talking isn't going to help me. It's just not. Though, now that I think about it, it might help Leif.

"I haven't told anyone else about this," I say.

His gaze jumps to my face.

"I've had this dream a couple of times since I woke up where I can't move, but the light is slowly disappearing and the dark is setting in. I know something bad is in the shadows, but there's nothing I can do." I take the pan off the heat and measure out and mix in the rest of the ingredients. It's easier to confess a weakness without making eye contact. To say the words aloud and let out my messy insides without exactly listening. "It's so frustrating and scary. I wake up in tears, trying to get my body to move, feeling something creeping closer and closer and the dread is just horrible."

"You think it's from when you were in a coma?"

"Who knows?" I shrug. "It's as good a guess as any. No one can tell me what the brain does and doesn't process in that situation. Everyone's experience seems a little different. How awake or aware they are. If they dreamed or not. How much time passed for them, if any."

"You read about some cases?"

"Yeah," I say. "Doctors and nurses at the hospital and rehab talked to me about them sometimes too. One woman had a car accident like me and dreamed the entire three weeks she was in a coma that she was driving to work. Couldn't figure out what was taking so long. Another man dreamed he was happily married and had this whole wonderful life. But when he woke up none of it was true. It was all just gone."

"That must have been fucking horrible."

"Right? It would be heartbreaking. To expect to wake up to this beautiful life, but it's all gone."

His face stills. "That's a little like your situation in a way."

"Yeah," I say. "I guess so. Anyway . . ."

"But you didn't see anything in all that time you were lying there in the hospital?"

I shake my head. "No, not that I remember. I just woke up and all this time had passed. It didn't feel real. Didn't seem possible. It was the day of the accident and then it was seven months later. Boom. Time just disappeared on me."

"So we're both a little messed up," he says.

"We went through a hell of a thing. Nearly got killed. Shouldn't we be a bit messed up?"

He says nothing for so long that I finally look up. While I worked, he'd been stacking the dirty items in the dishwasher. I thoroughly approve. His expression isn't haunted now, more contemplative. His gaze narrowed, and jaw set. "I think you're right."

I just nod. "Been meaning to ask, what did you read to me when you were coming into the hospital to visit?"

"Oh." His cheeks brighten and he looks away. "Clem was in charge of buying the books. She didn't want to plant any bad or dark ideas inside your head. We thought it was best to keep things reasonably light and happy. Your mom also made some suggestions."

"Okay."

He just nods.

"What was the book?"

He clears his throat. "I was reading you *The Twilight Saga*."

"Really?"

"Yeah. I was worried it might be a bit dark, what with all the vampires. But Clem told me how they're actually all sparkly and I figured it would be okay. At least, you never complained about it until now."

"I'm not complaining."

"How long do these need to cook for?"

"If you'd like to do the honors and spread the batter in the pan?" I carefully hand him the saucepan and spoon. "Around half an hour or so."

"Who gets to lick the spoon?"

"Knock yourself out."

There's a childlike gleam in his eyes. "You're too kind."

"Leif, I loved those books when I was a teenager," I say, a weird kind of warmth forming in my chest area. "Watched the films so many times. Listening to you reading them would have been like revisiting old friends."

His smile is the most beautiful thing I've ever beheld. It makes me feel warm inside. "Good," he says. "I'm glad."

There are four people waiting at the front desk and Ed is on the phone when I arrive at the tattoo parlor the next day. A distinct vibe of chaos is in the air, the place is so busy. On one of the massage-type tables, a lady waits with her calves exposed for the inking.

Leif rushes to the front from out back, a tablet in his hand. "He's got a few spots open in three or four weeks' time," he says to a young man standing at the front desk.

I take a seat on the velvet chaise and wait with the container of brownies on my lap.

The young man hems and haws over what day to pick. Asking twice if Leif is positive there's nothing sooner. It seems weird to me that someone would be in such a hurry to do something permanent to their body. Someone needs to tell the dude that patience is a virtue.

In the end, Leif says with a strained smile, "You can go somewhere else if you're in a rush, man. That's all Ed's got available in the next month. What'll it be?"

There's no sign of Tessa today. Just Ed and Leif. And Leif left the apartment in such a rush he forgot to take the brownies to share at work. Since my therapy session got cancelled this morning, I figured I'd take a walk and deliver them. Only doing this, stopping by his work this way, feels a little like pretending to be his significant other. Like when I used to drop things off for Ryan now and then. But sharing a place with Leif is temporary. This is a transitional time. And it wouldn't make sense to forget that and get carried away. To get dependent on him, or the idea of him, somehow. I would be fine on my own. That's the truth of the matter.

Meanwhile, thinking about the divorce works spectacularly well as a mental cold shower for when my thoughts run wild. Ryan tried to fight me over some potted plants I alone have kept alive over the past couple of years. He did not win. The idiot.

In front of me, the phone keeps ringing and the people keep coming and the two of them are obviously slammed. Waiting customers are given a personal information and medical form to fill out. Questions are asked and books full of examples of tattoos are looked through.

"Hey," Leif says eventually, joining me on the chaise after

things have calmed a little. "You brought the brownies. Thank you!"

"You're welcome."

He opens the container to take a peek inside. "Awesome. Thanks for keeping me company last night. But you don't have to do that every night, you know?"

"You have trouble sleeping every night?"

In lieu of a response, he draws me closer and kisses my forehead. He probably means it in a friendship-type way, but talk about swoon. My knees go weak. On the inside, I have turned to goo. Also, my face is warm where he kissed me. I hope I'm not blushing. Only it seemed more sincere than his usual flirty wink. A more heartfelt showing of real-life actual affection. Now I'm just overthinking it. Not good. This infatuation needs to die a quiet death before I start putting pictures of him up on the back of my bedroom door. Carving our initials into some poor innocent tree or some other such nonsense.

The drill-type noise of Ed's tattoo gun now accompanies the music. It's Halsey, I think. Another song I don't know that probably came out while I was in a coma.

"Still no receptionist?" I ask.

"Eh. Latest apprentice gave up and went back to art school." He scratches his chin. "We'll find someone eventually."

"Is it always this busy first thing?"

"Tends to be, yeah."

"My therapy got cancelled this morning. I can stay for a few hours and help out."

He pauses. "Anna, you don't have to—"

"I know I don't have to. I want to."

"Well, I'm not going to say no." He stands, heading over to the counter. "Let me give you a quick rundown."

And that's how I start doing a couple of hours at Larsen and Sons Tattoo Parlor a few days a week. Ed is beyond grateful and Leif and Tessa are happy to have me around. Delighted to have some time during the day where they don't have to juggle the phone. It's a big change from my work at the inn. There, I was the woman in the office out back keeping everything running behind the scenes. But here I'm front and center. It's a steep learning curve and I ask a lot of questions, but everyone's patient with me and the extra bit of income is nice. So is feeling useful again.

In no time at all I can give the appropriate responses to all the basic questions, such as do tattoos hurt? Depends on the placement and your own pain tolerance. How much does it cost? Each tattoo artist has a different hourly rate and if you're inclined to haggle, then please recall that you'll be wearing this piece of art for the rest of your life. Don't make me smack some sense and respect into you. Are they safe? We follow all recommended safety precautions, but please make sure you're honest with regards to any medical conditions. What should I get? I can't answer this question for you. Where should I get it? I don't want to answer this question for you.

No one minds me being somewhat salty in response to the last one. Or if they do, they keep it to themselves. Leif raised his brows, but got on with his work with a smile. And this is the kind of reaction I can handle.

I am the no-nonsense woman on the front desk and I like it. I like it a lot. I like the control, and I like getting dressed and going somewhere that has nothing to do with the accident or its aftereffects. I like my new life.

"What's with his face?"

"What do you mean?"

"Just look at him," says Leif, hand waving vaguely at the screen.

Yeah. He's still not talking sense. So in response, I shove some popcorn in my mouth. Popcorn is never not a good idea.

It's around midnight and we're watching a movie. *The* movie. *Twilight*. Blueberry muffins that we made earlier are cooking in the oven and all is right and good. Leif's baking skills are improving with the almost nightly practice he's had over the last week. Clem and Ed have declared me the best neighbor ever on account of all the delicious goodies they're now getting so my ass doesn't get too out of control. Cooking seems to relax Leif when he gets all wound up and over-awake at night, and I couldn't say no to the possibility of a cookie if my life depended on it. Therefore, we keep on baking.

"Good soundtrack," says Leif, holding the bowl of popped goodness closer to me. He's a nice man. "But honest to God, Edward looks low-key tortured all the time."

"You have to understand that her blood smells like the best food ever to him. She's the ultimate temptation and he's like a vegan vampire or whatever."

"What? She smells like tacos?"

"Exactly. Bella's blood is the best tacos you've ever had in your life."

"Huh." He contemplates this. "I had some really great fish

tacos this one time in Mexico when I was twenty-two. They were amazing. Life altering, really. Served with just the right amount of lime juice."

"That's it then. Bella's blood smells like the fish tacos from your vacation in Mexico when you were twenty-two," I explain. "And Edward is mad keen on tacos with just the right amount of lime juice and he's desperate to sample, but he can't. Because if he starts, he might not stop."

"Got it. Is that generally considered heroic, wanting to eat the heroine?"

"Not this kind of eating, no."

We both look at each other and start giggling like idiots.

Then he stops. "Them being teenagers is a concern, however."

"Well, yeah, but his character is over a hundred years old."

"Pervert."

"It is one hell of an age gap, I'll give you that. I was a teenager when I first started watching this," I say. "But a lot of adults are into YA. It's nothing to be ashamed of. They're good stories. No sexy times actually happen until she's over eighteen in the second-to-last movie, so . . ."

"You're going to make me watch all of these movies, aren't you?" he asks, not sounding particularly worried about the prospect.

"Yes." It's the simple truth.

He just nods.

And then it happens. The sound of the vehicle skidding across the road makes some animal forgotten part of my brain react. Fight-or-flight coming to the fore. My heart hammers inside my chest. The sight of the vehicle careening toward her . . . *shit*. I jerk back hard in my seat as on screen, Edward saves

Bella from being crushed by a moving vehicle. It hadn't even occurred to me. That this sort of thing would come up now and
then and freak me the hell out. Dammit.

"You okay?" he asks, gaze concerned.

Every muscle in me from top to toe is drawn tight and I've
broken out in a cold sweat. "Yeah. I just . . . I forgot about that
bit. But it's fine. I'm fine."

"We can change movies if you want."

"No. It's all right. Wait. Are you okay?" After all, I'm not
the only one with issues relating to motor vehicle accidents. "Do
you want to turn it off?"

He shrugs. "I'm fine."

That's it. That's all he gives me. But somehow, I don't quite
believe him. There's a certain tension to him too. Unless he's
feeding off of my angst. Fuck, I wish I had a psychology degree
around about now.

"Are you sure?" I ask.

"Yep."

"Okay." I settle back, taking nice, deep even breaths. What
am I going to do? Freak out every time there's a car crash on
TV? Nope. I will not let my fears rule me. Nor can I force Leif
into confronting whatever may or may not be hiding inside his
head. That's his trauma to process in his own time.

On screen, Bella is surrounded by her concerned friends
before being examined by a doctor. The bland walls and hospital beds and everything are an immediate downer.

"Yuck," I say. "If I never see the inside of a hospital again
I'll die happy."

He sighs and settles back into the couch without a word.
More proof that the screechy vehicle sounds got on his nerves

too. Leif is a chatterer. He always has something to say. Which makes me wonder if the violence upsets him also. Seeing his sister-in-law left bleeding out on the ground after a knife attack would have to stick inside your head. The sight of so much blood and pain must linger in the worst way possible. And it happened pretty much right outside our front door.

It didn't even occur to me when I was choosing the movie to beware of blood and violence. I'm a lousy friend. Leif has been through a crazy amount in the last couple of years. I'm impressed he's managed to hold himself together as well as he has.

"Do you think having your dad as the local sheriff would mean you were more or less inclined to get into mischief?" he asks.

"I don't know. Depends on how deep your need to rebel runs, I guess," I say. "We really can put on something else if you'd prefer."

"Nuh."

Okay. "Oh, they're having their first fight slash mild disagreement. How dramatic."

"Much tension."

"Such romance."

And because I'm watching him out of the corner of my eye, I catch his frown a minute or two later. "Is it really considered romantic to break into a girl's room and stand in the corner watching her sleep?"

"Let's remember that this is a fantasy," I say. "We know that she's fundamentally safe with Edward because he's the hero. We can trust him to always do the right thing with her. Therefore we can imagine being wanted in that all-consuming way to such a thrilling degree by a hot dude while disregarding any and all real-life stalkers-breaking-and-entering concerns."

A grunt from him.

I curl my feet up underneath me. So I spent the better part of my teenage years overthinking *Twilight*. It made me happy.

"You once commented that you thought I was hot," he says.

"Did I?"

"Am I to therefore believe that you would find it thrilling for me to watch you sleep?"

"I'm pretty sure you have better things to do than watch me sleep." My heart did not start beating faster at his words. It's just still riled up over the car thing. "Like seeing to your belly-button lint issue."

With a frown, he tugs up his T-shirt. Oh good God, what have I done? He sits there beside me, showing off his amazing body like it's nothing. And of course I cannot look away. I'm so weak and wanton these days. It's dreadful.

"My belly button is perfectly clean." He sniffs with disdain. "Where are you getting your information from, lady?"

"It was a joke. Stop it." I tug on his shirt with a scowl. "Cover yourself."

"Why? What's wrong with my body?" He smirks. Because he knows damn well he's perfection. The asshole. I hate him and I keep having this insane urge to have sex with him, but we're really just friends. Just. Friends.

For so many reasons.

"Nothing," I say. "I made a joke and you took it too far."

"Did not."

"Did too," I say, because mature competent adult.

"Did not."

"I am rising above your petty and juvenile behavior," I say, then seize control of the bowl of popcorn. Maybe if I keep my mouth full I'll refrain from saying anything stupid ever again, or at least for a little while. A girl can dream. But first, "House rule number one. People in central areas of the residence must be fully dressed at all times."

"But what if I'm exercising and I get hot so I have to take my shirt off and inadvertently show some skin?"

"I don't see how that would be inadvertent."

"Gleaming, sweaty skin," he drawls. "I really do get over-heated while exercising. Please consider my request."

I think it over and sigh. He sort of has a point regarding getting hot while exercising. But he's also sort of being the Lord of Mixed Signals.

And then he opens his mouth and says, "It's not like you haven't seen it all before anyway."

"What? What are you talking about?" I ask. "I haven't seen *it all*."

"The other night you saw me without my shirt."

"But that's not *it all*."

He lifts one shoulder. "Eh."

I sigh. The man knows nothing.

"The upper body is usually the most interesting aesthetic part on most people," he says. "Tattooing and other various activities has taught me that."

I look to heaven. No help is forthcoming. "Let me guess, you're a breast man? That's where this idiocy is coming from."

"Breasts are good."

"So are thighs and asses and junk."

The corner of his lip quirks in amusement like he's gotten

me to say a dirty word. Inside the heart of every man is a twelve-year-old boy. One who wants to talk smut and make fart jokes. And I'm reasonably certain that at least this time I didn't start the sex talk. At least, not intentionally. Also he's giving me a strange, speculative sort of look.

"What?" I ask.

"I was just thinking."

God help me. "What?"

"You probably don't want to hear it."

"Okay." This whole line of discussion feels beyond dangerous. "Shut up and watch the movie then."

He holds his peace for all of approximately half a second. "I was just going to say that if you—"

"No," I say, adamant. "You're right, I don't want to hear it. Because whatever comes out of your mouth next is guaranteed to make things even more awkward."

"Yeah, but awkward is kind of what we do best." He tilts his head, watching me out of the corner of his eye. "Think about it, young Anna. We're always having strange little overly honest conversations. It's refreshing. People clutter their talking up with so much nonsense these days. The cool thing to say. The smart thing to say. The polite thing to say. But never the honest and open thing. The thing that's really on their mind. Why is that?"

"Probably because they don't want to get hurt or hurt other people. They don't want to look foolish or leave themselves open to being misconstrued," I say. "I don't know. Communication is tricky. There's lots of ways it can go wrong."

"Hmm."

"Hmm, what?"

"I think there's a level of trust and understanding here between us that's beautiful, is all."

I have nothing. He's right and it is beautiful. Our irreverent conversations far and away eclipse the conversations Ryan and I used to have. Maybe it's a passing thing. Maybe Leif and I will drift apart. But right here, right now is something special. Though I'm still not going to tell him everything. There are plenty of thoughts that I don't need to share. All the same, I can't keep the happy off my face.

"Don't you think?" he asks.

"Yes. I do."

And he just smiles.

CHAPTER FIVE

HERE'S A SORT OF FORCED INTIMACY THAT COMES WITH sharing a space with someone. For instance, Leif has a habit of walking from the bathroom to his bedroom post shower clad in only a towel. Then there's the wandering in, dripping sweat and half naked, fresh from a run with Ed. Not to forget how rumpled and lost he looks first thing in the morning. I've taken to shoving a cup of coffee into his hand and forgoing all conversation for the first half an hour or until his brain has come online. It's best for everyone.

None of this is helpful for my crush on him. But I can handle it. This crush is a bounce. It's a distraction from everything happening in my life. It's not serious. And I am not protesting too much. I'm just keeping things straight inside my head. Sometimes you need to have a stern talk to yourself. I seem to be doing this on an hourly basis. Let's not question why.

It is, however, interesting noting how much more time Leif and I spend together as opposed to the life I had with Ryan. He was always off to the gym or working late. Something I'd grown accustomed to at the time. Though it kind of makes me wonder about how healthy our relationship was really. Guess the rose-colored glasses are well and truly off. But I'm not dwelling on Ryan either. I'm doing my exercises and rebuilding my life, which now includes working at the tattoo parlor. I'm getting my shit together. Romance and menfolk are nice and all; however, they're by no means a necessity.

Which goes nowhere toward explaining why I'm sitting at the table with my dinner waiting for Leif to make an appearance. Because we're not hanging out together tonight. Not even a little.

When he finally walks out of his bedroom, it's in a black pair of jeans, a black button-down shirt, and black boots. His hair is tied back and his gaze is not exactly happy. Honestly, I can't read him. There's a line between his brows, but none on his forehead, so his anxiety levels are probably slightly above normal maybe.

"You look good," I say, holding a rib in my sticky fingers. Barbeque was given to us by God. It's a fact. Add collard greens and cornbread and you've basically got nirvana. Living in the middle of town and having access to all of the delivery in all the land is working out well for me, if not my bank account.

He smiles. "You're a mess."

"There's only one way to eat ribs, and that is with your whole mouth and soul."

"I see." He crosses to the kitchen, pulls out a clean towel, and wets it beneath the sink before returning to the table. "Look here."

Ever so carefully, he cleans off my face.

I laugh. "I feel like a child."

"Yeah. Well. You don't look like one if that helps." And there's a warmth in his eyes that kills me.

"Thank you." I look away for a moment. "So you're all ready for your hot date?"

He shrugs.

"What's wrong?"

"I hate getting set up. It's so fucking awkward." He leaves the damp towel at my elbow on the table for later use.

"I hear you. Happily, I'm not at that stage yet," I say. "Tell me about her."

"Ah, friend of Clem's. Works at a place opposite the book-store. That's about all I know."

"Is it a double date or . . ."

"Yeah. Which is just more pressure to connect, you know? Under normal circumstances you can meet, have a drink, fig-ure you have nothing in common or there's nil attraction and go your separate ways all in under thirty minutes," he says. "But getting dragged along on a double date means you're stuck there for the whole night whether you're interested or not."

I nod.

"Ed gave me the 'you hardly ever go out and socialize any-more' lecture followed by the 'it won't kill you so stop being a little bitch about it' speech."

"Oh. Sounds involved. Still, it must be nice having siblings that care about you."

"It is. And I know I'm being negative as all hell."

"You're allowed to feel how you feel. This is our safe space, after all."

"But there's no point to feeling how I feel, because short of faking my own death I've got to go." He sighs. "So I might as well pull my head out of my ass and get on with it. Who knows, it might be fun."

"Well said and bravely done."

"Thank you. I'm going to think of it as quality time with Ed and Clem with the possibility of something more."

There is no twinge of jealousy messing with my insides. It's just gas or something.

He rolls up the sleeves on his shirt, revealing his strong forearms. "What are you up to tonight, you little carnivore?"

"I haven't decided yet. Maybe call Mom and Briar and catch up with them. Put on a moisturizing mask and have a glass of wine. Just going to chill."

"Sounds nice. Don't watch any more *Twilight* until I'm back."

"I wouldn't dare."

One side of his mouth quirks up. "Who will Bella choose, the vampire or the werewolf?"

"I'll never tell."

"I'll just have to wait and see. Still, it's a good thing we reconnected. We only got halfway through the third book when I was reading to you in the hospital. If you'd never tracked me down, I would have just lived the rest of my life with this faint cloud of unresolved drama hanging over me. On my deathbed my final words would have been 'But was it Edward or Jacob?'" He winks. "Later."

And he's gone. On a date. Okay. Great. This is all completely normal and I'm fine with it. I am.

FIVE HOURS LATER . . .

"Anna? Baby? What are you doing?"

His big black boots appear at my side. "Cleaning."

"And that requires your upper body to be wedged underneath the kitchen sink?" His voice echoes around the confines of the otherwise silent main room. The music stopped a while back and I hadn't bothered to put on another playlist. I had better things to do.

"Yes," I say.

Nothing from him.

Like it's weird to spray and wipe down pipes or something. "I'm not sure anyone's ever cleaned back here. It's really dusty."

"You're probably right."

"How did the double date go?" I ask, trying to turn to look back at him, only it doesn't really work with my upper body inside the cupboard. Maneuvering is also difficult with a spray bottle of cleaning stuff and rag taking up my hands. Sometimes my coordination is off when I get tired. Such is life.

"Will you—can you come out here, please? It's hard to take you seriously when I'm talking to your buttocks."

"Um . . ."

"Let me help."

"Okay."

He grips me around the waist and pulls me out nice and slow. And I'm kneeling at his feet with my cleaning implements, which is never a good look. Dust-stained old tee and yoga pants only enhance my image.

He crouches down at my side. "So. Anna. What's going on?"

"Nothing."

"It looks like you scrubbed and bleached every inch of the condo."

"Sort of. Yeah. Well, no. Mostly just the main room and

111

kitchen. I don't think I'll get to the bathroom tonight. I'm starting to run out of steam."

"What happened to chilling with a face mask and a drink?"

"I did that too. Then I got bored and figured, why not?"

"Okay." His tongue plays behind his cheek, but his eyes are serious. "Do you find cleaning relaxes you?"

I think it over. "No. Not really."

"Right." His gaze runs over my yellow rubber gloves before he too sits on the floor. "Talk me through this."

"It's nothing. Everyone has their quirks," I say, starting to feel distinctly judged. As if rage and/or anxiety cleaning wasn't a thing. "You haven't told me how your date went."

"It was fine. She was nice. The food was good."

"Nice? That's all you've got?"

He tugs the hair tie out, letting it all hang loose. "We went dancing and . . . I didn't hate it."

"Whoa. Gush about the girl, why don't you?"

A grunt. "I don't know. Maybe I'm just going through an extended no-interest-in-dating period. There's nothing wrong with that."

"There is nothing wrong with that."

"You know, I don't even miss sex that much, now that I come to think about it. Maybe the accident damaged by libido. And I'm fine with my own company. Or I have the guys from work, my family, and you to hang out with," he says. "It's not like I've become a hermit or something."

"Fair enough."

"I'm more worried by your cleaning rampage."

I set down the cleaning implements and wriggle around on my butt until I can lean back against a kitchen cupboard door.

Assorted muscles in me ache from all of the hard work and I do not blame them one bit. "Don't be. My brain was busy, so I figured my hands may as well be too. Get rid of all the excess energy, you know?"

"What was your brain busy with, or is that private?"

Good question. Not one I particularly wish to answer, however. "Mom does this sometimes. It's part of why I've been known to call her house the museum. Everything is immaculate and cleaned to the nth degree. Guess I inherited it from her."

A nod. "You're deflecting. But I'm going to let that go because it's obviously none of my business and you'll talk about it or not when you're ready."

"Thank you."

"No problem." He smiles. "The place is so clean. Want to mess it up by baking something?"

I grin. "Sure."

"Let me get this right, you want to express yourself by getting a large swastika tattooed on your head? That's what you want?"

The big bald white man smiles down at me in a creepy manner.

Out of nowhere, Ed appears at my side. He doesn't say anything, he just stands there. And while I don't need it, I appreciate the support just the same. If I can survive a collision with another car and being cut out of my vehicle and playing Sleeping Beauty for seven months while my life goes to hell, I can handle this repugnant asshole.

"No," I say.

"I'm not talking to you anymore," says the man. "I'm dealing with him."

Ed crosses his arms. "What she said."

"Are you fucking with me?" The guy sneers.

"No," says Ed. "We are not fucking with you. Fucking with you would be agreeing to your request and then tattooing a pony onto your head the moment you're in the chair."

"I'm afraid Larsen and Sons Tattoo Parlor is unable to meet your needs. And that's because your needs are gross and wrong and you should be ashamed of them." I tap a pen against the counter. "Leave now, please."

His expression morphs into fury and he slams his hand down on the reception desk, making the glass case rattle before about-facing and striding out. What a bully. Honestly.

"Get the hell out of here!" Ed shuts and locks the door after the man. Just to be careful, I guess. "Anna, are you okay?"

"Yeah." I'm shaking, but fine. Random violence happening in my face has a habit of freaking me out. Or maybe it's just confrontations in general. They kind of make me want to hurl. But I didn't and that's a win. I told the asshole off. Go, me.

Tessa just keeps on working at her station. But Leif's tattoo gun turns off and I give him a wave to let him know I'm fine. No one needs to rush to my rescue, for heaven's sake. This is the problem with men like Ed and Leif, a protective streak a mile wide. Sometimes I love it, that he cares so much, but sometimes it gets in the way.

"I'm real sorry. Every now and then we get some dumbass asking for something offensive or just morally messed up and have to tell them no," he says. "Sorry you had to deal with that."

"It's okay. I'm okay. Really."

Which is about when there's a rapping on the tattoo parlor door. Because today isn't promising to be interesting enough, apparently. A familiar, neatly presented blond woman stands on the other side. Celine. Talk about morally messed up. She looks paler than normal, with dark circles beneath her eyes. Definitely not glowing.

Apparently this bright, sunny morning is peak time for confrontations.

"You have got to be kidding me." I stride across the entry floor, flick back the lock, and jerk the heavy old wooden and glass door open. I don't stand back and let her in. Forget niceties. "What do you want?"

"We need to talk."

"About?"

She takes a deep breath, her hands balled into fists. "I heard you were working here and the thing is, you haven't officially resigned from your position at the inn. Legally, you're still employed by us."

I blink.

"We put you on leave when the accident happened and that's the ongoing status of your employment. You can't just start working somewhere else without giving us notification." Her hand rests on the small swell of her belly. I should maybe be over it by now. Her and Ryan and the baby and everything. But the truth is, on some level, it still hurts. "That's not right, Anna. You can't just do that. And to go work in a tattoo parlor of all places. You can't be serious."

"Celine, you fucked my husband."

She clicks her tongue. "Today of all days, surely you're ready to move on."

115

"I was, you know. Right up until you showed up here." I cock my head. "Just take a moment and let these words sink in. You fucked my husband. You, my boss and one of my best friends, fucked Ryan, my husband."

Her gaze rests on the ground.

"Did you really think I'd just come back to the inn and everything would be the same as it was before?" I ask. "What did you possibly hope to achieve coming here?"

"W-what do you mean? I'm just—"

"No, really. Why are you here?" And Leif's tattoo gun is still silent. I turn and again wave a hand at him to carry on with his business. To trust me to take care of mine. As sick as this sort of thing makes me, I'm a big girl. I can handle it on my own. "Well, Celine?"

"I'm trying to tell you that you still have a job with us. A job that you loved, if you'll recall?" she asks, voice tense, accusing almost.

"You're right, I did. I'll be sure to add that to the list of things you ruined for me. Because there is no possible way I'm coming back to work for you now."

"It doesn't have to be like this," she said through clenched teeth. "I'm trying to help you."

And while I'm probably being a bit of an asshole, I can't help but feel that it's about time I started pushing back. I'm done with being nice. Finished with saying the polite thing or nothing at all. Especially if someone is so keen on bringing the fight to me. "No, you're not. I'm not sure what you're up to, exactly. But it has nothing to do with helping me. I'd guess you're propping up your ego. Doing your best to convince yourself you're a stand-up person and all that."

"We used to be friends."

"As I pointed out literally thirty seconds ago when explaining my grievance about you fucking my husband, yes. We used to be friends. But we sure as hell no longer are."

"Anna . . ."

"Did I really used to be this much of a doormat that you thought coming here like this would get you somewhere?" I ask, genuinely curious. "What else are you going to take off my hands? You already have Ryan. I'd imagine you'll be setting up house with him any day now, huh? Moving into my former home. Then you'll probably start pushing for the engagement ring. It's like you'll be living my life. Or my former life."

At this, she turns away. Guilty as sin.

"And you're welcome to it. You really are."

"It's not like that," she hisses.

"No?"

"I came here to try and help you."

"Thing is, I don't need your help. And it doesn't matter how many times you tell yourself that you're trying to help me, it won't make it the truth," I say. "I'm sorry if you're having a hard time with the pregnancy. I really am. But I'm not sorry if you feel like shit about yourself. There are consequences to what you did. I'm never going to open my arms and say that it's all right and all is forgiven, Celine. That's never going to happen. I am never going to want anything to do with either of you ever again."

Her lips are a fine white line. "So you don't want your job back. That's what you're saying."

"Not even a little. If you really want to do me a favor, don't come near me again."

"Fine." And she too stomps off. Holy hell.

117

I let the door close and take a deep breath, head back to the reception counter. What a day. What a life.

"You told her," says Tessa with a smile that's all sharp teeth. I really like her.

"Didn't know you were getting a floor show when they hired me, did you?" I laugh with all of the self-consciousness inside of me. "Anyway."

Meanwhile, Leif has gotten up from where he's been tattooing some dude's shoulder and wanders my way. There's a strange sort of expression on his face. One I can't read.

"What?" I ask.

He doesn't touch me on account of wearing gloves, but he leans in until our faces are close together. Until it's just me and him and nothing else exists. My foolish heart gives a weird little jolt at the nearness.

"I'm going to hug you later," he says.

"I'll look forward to it."

"That was very fight club of you," he says in a voice little more than a whisper. Just for the two of us. "You didn't back down or run away. And you didn't let her get away with anything or put her shit on you."

I shrug. It's hard to think with him so close.

"I'm proud of you."

"Thanks, I think," I say, keeping my voice equally low. My eyes get suspiciously wet at his praise. Though it has been an emotional day. Which just goes to show that I can explain away anything given half a chance. What a superpower.

"No problem."

"No problem," I agree, only I'm about as wrong as you can

get. Because there is a problem. A huge one. And it's getting bigger and messier by the day.

"You're dressed up," is the first thing Leif says, his eyes wide. He sets his motorbike helmet on the side table, and his leather jacket is hung over the back of one of my dining room chairs. "Wow."

"This is a momentous occasion."

"It is? I was going to ask if you wanted to come to the bar for the regular Saturday evening giant-Bloody-Mary-with-lobster-roll combo. But I'm sensing you already have plans." He accepts a glass of champagne, his gaze still roving all over me. There's a mix of pleasure and surprise on his face and I can't help but preen just a little.

Truth be known, the plunging neckline on my ankle-length black silk gown is rather beguiling. I bought it for a New Year's Eve party a few years back and it still fits okay. Tonight just struck me as being a smoky eyes, neutral lips, and hair blown out kind of occasion. A time for thinking and drinking and dancing. So as soon as I got back from my divorce attorney's office, that's what I did. My feet are bare because comfort matters, but my toenails are painted black to match. Harry Styles is on the stereo, I have a buzz happening, and all is well.

"You know," I say, holding my champagne high. Not my first glass, either. God help my liver. "People put all this effort into celebrating weddings, yet they don't put even half the energy into observing a divorce."

He raises a brow. "It's official?"

"Signed the papers this afternoon."

"Huh." He clinks his glass against mine. "You didn't tell me that was today."

"I wasn't sure how I felt about it until now."

Nothing from him.

"I was thinking of doing a bit of crafting with the certificate when it arrives. Some flowery stamps, maybe," I say. "A little glitter. Really make it special, you know? Bring out the love and joy inherent in the document."

Still nothing from him.

"I am twenty-seven years old and divorced," I say, testing the words. "I am a single woman once again."

He sips the champagne. "Yes you are. You're finally free. Is 'congratulations' the right thing to say?"

"Sure. Divorce is about two people bravely committing to the romantic idea that they can make it on their own. It's quite empowering really."

"Then congratulations, Anna."

"Thank you. I'm glad it's over."

And he's being so damn cautious. It's right there in his wary gaze. "I bet you are."

"I'm not going to burst into tears or something," I say. "There's no need to look so scared. Out of all of the emotional trauma I've experienced this year, tonight actually feels like a good thing."

"I don't mind. Cry if you want or need to. I'm not going anywhere. I'm not afraid of you." He downs half of the glass of champagne. "You know, this isn't half bad."

"Glad you approve. I thought if we were going to celebrate, then really only French champagne would do."

A small smile.

"I'm okay, Leif. I promise."

"You've been through a lot of shit."

"So have you," I say. "We both deserve good things."

He smiles for real this time. "I'll drink to that."

"You need a refill." I grab the bottle out of the bucket of ice on the kitchen counter and perform my duties as host of this very small party. A wedding wake, if you will. A marriage memoriam. There's even cheesecake in the fridge for later, because a party is nothing without cake.

"How much have you had to drink?" he asks, giving me a curious glance.

"We may be onto our second bottle, here," I answer. "Briar and I FaceTimed a couple of glasses' worth earlier. A bid-adieu-to-the-cheating-bastard kind of thing. Will you dance with me?"

"I'd be honored."

The music changes to Leon Bridges and he slides his arms around my waist. I set one hand on his shoulder, the other still holding onto my drink. We sway in time to the music. It's so easy with him. So comfortable. Also, Leif is tall and firm and smells nice. The perfect companion for this sort of thing. He's ridiculously handsome up close like this. Lady-part-tingling male beauty. And I get to put my hands on him in a purely friendly manner. Lucky me.

"No man-hating angry music," he notes.

"Nope." I smile. "Don't get me wrong, I went through an intense period of despising your gender. But that kind of emotion isn't sustainable long term. Not for me, at least. Especially not with Celine involved in it up to her pretty little neck. Two people alone are responsible for this situation. No point throwing away the whole world over their misdeeds."

A grunt.

"I guess I still have my moments of rage," I say. "I mean, of course I do. It was a deeply shitty thing to have happen. But being pissed off for the rest of all time seems like it'll do me more harm than good."

He nods.

"I want to move on to bigger and better things. Be happy. And I can't do that if I'm letting this stuff drag me down."

"Sounds wise."

"You think so?" I ask.

"Yes."

I nod. "Not that I think I'll ever marry again."

He raises a brow. "No?"

"Nope. That is not on the agenda. Been there, done that, getting the divorce certificate."

"Why not?" he asks. "You might meet someone who makes your ex look like a sad excuse of a man. Someone who makes you deliriously happy."

"I might. One day . . ." I sigh. "But weddings are so big and expensive and stressful. And it's not like the vows necessarily mean a whole lot. I mean, why bother?"

"It's true. Words are cheap. That's why I recommend tattoos, because ink is forever."

"Hm." I think about this. "But can't you get tattoos erased now? Or at least redone?"

He shakes his head. "Not entirely. There's always a mark. No one gets to walk away free and clear."

"Is that a good thing?"

"Of course." He seems surprised by the question. "That's why we all do it. To have it carved into us in blood and skin and ink. To mark out something that's important enough to stay with us to the end. Something we can't change our mind about. Not like promises or wedding vows."

"I'll keep that in mind. Not that I wasn't a stunning bride. I wore this white strapless ball gown that was like a dream. The skirt was all done in box pleats," I say. "I looked like a walking, talking cake. It was glorious."

"I bet you were beautiful."

"Thank you." My smile is all things dreamy with a side order of tipsy. "I'd show you some photos, but I actually burnt most of them in Mom and Dad's barbeque a few months back. Another cathartic healing moment on the road to singledom."

"That's okay. You can draw me a picture sometime."

"Will do," I say. "But even if I met someone amazing who against all odds was actually trustworthy, I don't really see any benefit to having a wedding. Marriage clearly can't make up for qualities that aren't there to begin with. Love. Loyalty. Little things like that."

His hand presses lightly against my lower back. A comforting presence. "One day, I'm going to convince you that some relationships are in fact worthwhile and some people can be trusted. But right now, drunky Anna, I'm just going to let you babble."

"In vino veritas," I say. "Thank you for indulging my deep thoughts. And I wasn't ruling out relationships in their entirety."

"No?"

"No. Just being more realistic about future possibilities," I explain. "I think this is actually quite healthy of me, casting aside the childhood fairy tales of the perfect Prince Charming and so on."

Leif snorts. "The dude couldn't recognize the love of his life without her makeup on and a fancy dress. I mean, how great was Charming really?"

"You're talking about Cinderella, I take it?" I laugh.

"Yes. It's a stupid story. Shoe size is a poor indicator for choosing a life partner. Ask anyone."

"This is a valid point." I pause mid sway to take a sip of champagne. Ah. Bubbly nectar of the booze gods. Get inside me.

His gaze turns speculative.

"What?"

"I'm not sure if I should ask," he says.

"Go for it."

"All right. Did you really think Ryan was Prince Charming? I mean, really, really?"

I take a deep breath. "Yeah. I guess I did. I mean, he wasn't always a dick. Sure, he had his foibles, but things between us used to be generally pretty good."

"Generally pretty good," he repeats.

"Dude. Marriage isn't easy."

"I believe that."

"But maybe with the right person it should be," I say, thinking deep thoughts. "I don't know. He was the first person I ever slept with. He's the *only* person I've ever slept with. Sorry if that's too much information."

Leif just shrugs.

"It's one of the things that concerns me now and then, actually." I must be inebriated or I'd never say this sort of thing out loud. "In those dark and foolish moments of extreme self-doubt. What if Celine was better in bed than me? What if she made him howl at the moon while I was only rated an okay? What if in the end that was why he chose her?"

He frowns.

"'Could do better,'" I say in a somewhat plaintive voice. "I used to get that a lot in gym class at school. 'If only she would apply herself.'"

"I'm pretty sure acing gym class doesn't automatically mean you've got mad skills in bed."

"But wouldn't it suggest that I had stamina and a certain flexibility?"

"I'm sure there are plenty of gym class flunkies who do just fine in the sack."

"Maybe."

"Enthusiasm trumps dexterity every time."

"Yeah. Think about it, though," I say. "I've only slept with one person. What do I know about going wild in bed, really? Maybe I need more practice. More hands-on experience."

"There's a lot I could say to that, but none of it is probably appropriate or helpful right now. Continue on with your ruminating." He swallows. "One question first. Was the sex even any good?"

I wrinkle my nose. "I think so. I mean, I have nothing to compare it to. Yet."

"Right."

"We were a couple within about five minutes after we met when I was a freshman." I take a moment to think it over. So many memories both good and bad. "I guess I didn't really know any better. Any high school boyfriends were fumbling-hands-type affairs. Boob gropes and valiant attempts to get their hands down my pants before curfew. Nothing serious."

He just nods.

"This is my chance to do some sexing and catch up to the rest of the population."

His brows rise. "That's your plan?"

"Why not?" I ask. "The last thing I need right now is a serious relationship. Therefore it's the perfect time to get me some."

"Okay." He looks away for a long moment. I'd pay serious money to know what's on his mind. "No serious relationships, huh?"

"Just like you."

"Sure," he says, sounding a little hesitant for some reason. "Whatever makes you happy."

"I guess we'll see what makes me happy. Currently I have no real idea."

"There's no rush. Take your time," he says, licking his lip. He has nice lips. "Ah, do you think you missed out on much, hooking up with him so early? In ways other than sex, I mean."

"Maybe. Probably." I think it over. "In a lot of ways I let him and our relationship define me. Not a mistake I'll make again. You've got to be your own person separate of any coupledom. Have your own life and interests. I mean, look at how many friends I lost in the divorce because the situation was awkward or made them worry about their own relationship on some level or me on my own just didn't fit with their perceptions of the world. I only made sense to them when I was part of a matching pair: 'Ryan and Anna.' It's ridiculous. I need to be my own person and have my own friends."

"I'll be your friend, single girl."

"Thank you. I'd be delighted to be your friend too."

Enough about me. Time for a change of subject. "What were you like when you were younger?"

"Virginal and virtuous." And he says it with such a straight face. "Those are the first two words that come to mind. Along with 'very.'"

"Right."

"Mostly I hung out in the back room at my uncle's tattoo parlor with Ed. We met all sorts of people. It was an education."

"I bet."

"We'd draw tattoo design ideas and ask a million questions and generally get in the way," he says. "Our older brother, Niels, was the sporting type. He was big into football. And Ed was more artistic than me. He was always painting the walls of his bedroom and doing the emo artist thing. I was the loudmouth out of the three of us. Always cracking jokes and trying to woo the girls, but not always successful."

"I can see you as a little charmer."

"Ha. No. I had no game," he says. "It took me years to become the practiced lothario you see now before you."

"Ha."

"I'm ready and available to whisper dirty things in your ear whenever you're ready," he offers. "Free of charge even."

"That's very kind of you. I'll keep it in mind." I smile all serene-like because I am an amazing actress sometimes. "You never came close to getting married or settling down?"

He downs some champagne. "I've dated some great girls. Or women, I should say. And there was one or two that maybe made me want to keep things going. To explore something more . . . but in the end for various reasons it didn't work out."

"Guess it wasn't meant to be."

"Guess not."

"What reasons?" I ask, because booze is so great for

removing any and all social constraints. Like being polite and minding your own business even matters. Cheers!

"Ah, well, one was a tattoo artist that I met at a convention. We tried long distance for a while, but in the end she wanted to be in L.A. and I wanted to be here."

"Okay. That's sad, but inevitable. And the other?"

"This was back when Ed had just taken over the parlor and we were all working our asses off to make it a success," he says. "Joni couldn't handle the hours I was working. I mean, she had a point. She was going to school during the day and tending bar at night. We barely got to see each other."

"You really liked her?"

"We had a lot of fun together."

I frown. "Fun isn't an emotion. It tells me nothing about how you felt for this woman."

"It was ten years ago, Anna. That's a long time. I don't know how I felt."

"Hmm."

"What does that mean?" he asks. "What is 'hmm'?"

"Maybe if you can't remember how you felt, then moving on was the right answer."

His expression tenses as he gazes down at the next-to-non-existent space between us. Or maybe it's more about the neck-line of my dress. I'm showing a lot of skin and I do not care.

"You don't like my dress?"

His lips compress. "I love your dress."

"Then why so glum, my friend? This is, after all, a party."

"Nothing." He eases back a little. Just so our hips and chests are no longer touching. "Everything is great."

"Okay. If you say so." My brain is suddenly busy as can be.

"I kind of hijacked you the minute you walked in the door. If you'd rather go to the bar, I completely understand. It's your routine. Your end-of-the-workweek celebration. I can do the one-girl disco here just fine."

"What? And miss out on swilling champagne, slow-dancing, and watching *Twilight*?"

"Go, Team Edward."

"Eh," says Leif. "Not saying he doesn't have cool hair, but Jacob has all those rippling muscles."

"That's true. It's a hard choice." I smile. "Thank you."

"For what?"

"For being my friend."

His smile is slow and beautiful. "It's an honor."

CHAPTER SIX

D AY ONE OF BEING A SINGLE WOMAN GOES LIKE THIS. My head hurts and my mouth feels like death and my cell won't stop buzzing. It's so bad that it wakes up Leif, who's lying beside me. This is due to drunken late-night discussions that resulted in us both passing out on my bed.

We didn't mean to sleep together, it just happened. But nothing actually happened other than sleep.

"Make it stop," he mumbles, face embedded in a white Egyptian cotton pillow with a subtle decorative edging. One of my favorite sets. I choose not to care that they were an engagement gift. If I start letting the existence of Ryan and memories made with him define the value of my belongings then I'll be down to owning nothing. He got years of my life. He doesn't get to take another thing from me.

Meanwhile, Leif is not a morning person at the best of times and multiple bottles of champagne the night before can't be helping. In fact, I'm kind of amazed he's still beside me on the bed. I figured for sure he'd have been unable to sleep with someone nearby and have snuck out at some stage while I snored the passed-out drunken song of my people. But here he is. Amazing.

I reach over him to grab my cell off the bedside table. "Oh, God."

"What?"

"Not only have we slept half the day away, but my mother is inundating me with pictures and contact details of assorted single men in the area."

He opens one eye. "Already?"

"Yes. God help me," I say. "She's recommending that I try before I buy with a winking emoji. This is horrifying. What the hell has gotten into her?"

"What would her friends at church say about that?"

I shake my head. "I don't want to know. Part of me worries they put her up to it. That's an even more horrifying thought."

With much grumbling and groaning, Leif rolls onto his back. He's still in his faded black tee and blue jeans from last night. I'm still in my evening gown. When his gaze flicks over my chest region, I do a quick check to ensure the girls are covered. God bless double-sided tape. All necessities remain hidden. No such luck for my bird's nest of a hairdo. And the intimacy of waking up beside him is . . . a lot. But I can ignore that. No problem.

"Does Denise actually believe that you're going to rush out and get remarried without checking the fit first?" he asks, smothering a yawn.

"Checking the fit." I grin. "I've never heard it described that way. I don't know. Maybe she has doubts as to my ability to both find and go on a date. Perhaps she's gotten the hots for the idea of having grandkids. I don't know. Considering she didn't even like spending time with me when I was a child, I don't see how this is going to work." I scroll through the unending messages.

Mom's dedication sure is something. Something scary. "Oh. This one's a dentist. Score."

"Think of all those free fillings."

I snort. Talk about a meeting of dirty minds.

"May I?" asks Leif, holding out his hand.

I pass over my cell.

"Hold up. I know him," he mumbles.

"Really?"

"Yeah. He's got this amazing full-color serpent tattooed on his genitals. Hours of work, that."

"What?" I ask. "He has not. You're making that up."

"It's true. Ed did it himself," he says. "Got to hand it to your dentist, that sort of thing requires dedication. Especially getting your balls tattooed, you know? That's some sensitive skin. And so soft and wrinkly. Requires very careful handling. Don't even ask me about the amount of waxing you'd need to get done beforehand. Ouch."

I narrow my eyes. "You're lying."

"Of course I'm lying." He laughs. "Rest assured, I have no idea what, if anything, is on your dentist's dick. And even if I did, I'd be bound by professional confidentiality to never tell. But the fascination warring with distaste in your expression is fun to see, though."

"I wasn't doing anything," I say as I start typing out a text.

Me: Mother. No.
Mom: What do you mean?
Mom: I'm just trying to be supportive.
Me: Supportive is baking me a cake or buying me a bottle

of wine. Saying something kind. Supportive is not hunting up a bang for me the day after my divorce is finalized.

Mom: I'm just interested in your life.

Me: Be interested in my life out of the bedroom. Much less awkward.

Mom: Sex is a perfectly natural thing. Leif is right. You're so judgy.

"You told my mom I was judgy?" I ask, ever so slightly cranky. Or hung over. Possibly both.

"I need coffee," he says, sitting up and stretching. The way his biceps bulge during this process is frankly fascinating.

"I can't believe you said that to her."

He sighs. "Anna, I asked Denise where she thought you got your judgmental tendencies from. It was meant to be a joke, but I see the error of my ways now."

"You need to stop talking to my mom."

"No. I like Denise. She's funny."

"Yeah? Are you laughing with her or at her?"

"Now that hurts my feelings."

"I am perhaps somewhat overly defensive on this front. Sorry."

"Apology accepted. I'm laughing with her. That woman knows herself well. More than you give her credit for," he says. "And she doesn't take herself too seriously, either."

"Hmm."

"You have mommy issues," he says in a rough morning voice. "Fuck, my head hurts. Champagne is lethal."

"Yeah."

"No, really. I hurt in the weirdest places."

133

"Curtail your man pain. We're all suffering here," I say with a groan. "And I don't have mommy issues. Just some concerns about becoming her mixed with an innate fear of disappointing her brought on by being largely ignored throughout my childhood."

"Like I said. Mommy issues."

"Go make me coffee. Please. Pretty please?"

"Yes, ma'am." He heads for the door, but stops halfway. "I slept beside you."

I just smile.

"All night."

"Just figuring that out, huh?" I ask.

He scratches his head, his hair sticking out in every which direction. The difference between me and him is that he makes mornings look good. "Anna, I . . . wow. Wasn't actually sure that was possible anymore after Shannon and everything. But I didn't have a nightmare for once. Between you, the champagne, and your fancy bed linen, I actually spent an entire night asleep."

"You're going to be fine, Leif. You really are."

He frowns.

"She hurt you, but she didn't break you. And everything that happened is on her," I say, putting my heart and soul into the words. "You're a good person. One of the best people I've ever met. Be kind to yourself, Leif, and don't carry that around any longer. It's not your burden because you didn't do anything wrong. Let it go."

"Maybe."

"You can do better than that," I urge.

He gives himself a little shake. "Ugh. Okay. I guess you're right."

"I know I am. And it doesn't happen very often, so I really need to seize the moments when it does. Now go make me coffee."

"On it!"

I hope he's okay. He seems okay. People can do a hell of a lot of damage, intentional or otherwise. And the trauma Leif has been through is extreme. Speaking of which, this morning's domestic scene warms my wounded heart through and through. Though divorce hasn't left me as jaded and bitter as I'd expected. I actually feel okay about life and love. Hopeful, even. How could I not after spending the night dancing and drinking followed by waking up next to the object of my affections? So getting over my crush on Leif has been on my to-do list for a while now. Oh well.

Two Advil and a long hot shower fixes the bulk of my issues. My face is a smudged mess from sleeping in my makeup and I have a small zit on my chin. I really should know better. However, the divorce party was a great success. Everything is good. Right up until I walk out to find Leif hugging another woman in the kitchen.

Holy shit.

A beautiful woman with russet skin and long dark hair. She's like a piece of art with her heavy silver jewelry and red sheath dress. In my old jeans and a tee with my wet hair pulled back in a braid, I do not compare. And that's not just any old hug they're sharing. This isn't some brief pat on the back and you're good to go. They're so comfortable with each other's bodies. Because they're all but clinging to each other like the oldest and closest of friends or quite possibly a good deal more. It's a soul hug and I am left out in the cold. Here I thought it was me in particular who he liked hugging. But apparently the man is an equal opportunity hugger. Any girl will do.

I could swear someone just kicked me in the stomach.

Leif must sense me standing there staring because he opens his eyes and takes a small step back from the woman with an off-kilter kind of smile on his face. This is weird. I'm making this weird. Whatever expression is on my face right now needs to go. He was never mine and I have no right. I'm just surprised, is all. Really fucking surprised and kind of heartbroken.

"Anna," he says. "Hey, ah, this is Roshuane. An old friend of mine. Roshuane, this is my roommate, Anna."

And that's all we are. Roommates. Foolish of me not to get that through my thick skull by now.

The beautiful woman smiles and oh my God. I'm half in love with her myself. With jealousy slowly draining me of my will to live, I raise my hand in greeting. "Hi."

"Lovely to meet you, Anna," she says, her voice brimming with warmth. Because she has to be nice as well, doesn't she?

"Roshuane just got back in town," says Leif.

"We've got a lot to catch up on." And at this, she gives him a look that cannot be mistaken for anything but blatant carnal interest. Not that I blame her in the least. I harbor many of the same feelings for the man, after all.

Leif looks between his guest and me. The expression on his face seems to be on the verge of a smile, but again he's not quite sure if he should. He's allowed to be happy to see his friend and have sex with her if he so chooses. I'm just his roommate, after all.

"I'm heading out," I say, grabbing my purse off the side table. "I'll leave you guys to it. Nice to meet you, Roshuane."

"Anna . . ." Leif begins, but doesn't seem to know what to say for a minute. "Are you okay?"

"Yeah. I'm great," I lie with a smile. "See you later."

And I'm gone.

"Oh, yeah. They used to fuck like bunnies," confirms Clem. "We actually had to bang on the wall one night they were getting so loud."

Tessa squeezes her eyelids shut for a second. "Try some tact, yeah?"

I drain my cup of coffee. There's not enough caffeine in all of the world to get me through today. I'm just a big ball of hurt feelings. Along with a healthy dash of foolishness, of course.

The plan was to hide out for a few hours somewhere nearby. Call Briar and whine a while. Possibly retreat to the fallback position of my parents' house if necessary. But then I walked into a local café and Tessa, her partner Nevin, and their baby were there finishing brunch. After one look at my face, Tessa took me in hand. Apparently my fake smile sucks. Clementine was then summoned by text, and now here we are ensconced at a local bar. Just us girls.

"What?" asks Clem.

Tessa jerks her chin in my direction. "Anna has feelings for him. It's why I told you to get your ass down here."

I say nothing. Nothing needs to be said.

"You do? Shit," mutters Clem. "Sorry. It's funny. I wondered if there was something going on. But then you and he seemed to be all platonic and roommate-y, so I figured I was wrong."

"Platonic and roommate-y would have been the sensible option," I say, voice glum.

Tessa snorts. "Whoever said the heart was sensible?"

"That's true," says Clem. "Ed disliked me with much intensity, and with good reason, but I still stuck to the man like a tick. Couldn't help myself. I say hang in there, Anna. You're the only woman I've seen Leif spend quality time with since the accident. That has to mean something."

"No." I shake my head. "Well, yes, but it means we're friends. That's all. And I need to make peace with that because there's nothing wrong with being friends. I just have a bad habit of growing feelings for this guy and . . . gah."

"Do you know for sure Leif's not interested?" asks Tessa.

"Besides his sex friend showing up?" I ask.

"Besides that."

"Yes," I say. Because it's the truth. When I tried to kiss him he let me down as gently as possible. But it was still a rejection.

She frowns. "Damn."

"Never mind." I square my shoulders. "I have a part-time job that I enjoy. A nice condo that I share with a good friend. Lots of love and support. Life is good."

"Oh, by the way," says Tessa. "The accountant asked Ed to say thank you for getting the files up to date. Ed might forget, so this is me filling in on that front. We all hate doing admin work, so you're a godsend."

"Good. I'm glad."

"And we like you as a person," adds Clem.

"That's true," says Tessa with nil hesitation. "And we don't actually like many people."

Clem nods. "That's true. We're picky when it comes to people."

Oh my heart. I am being embraced by a new sisterhood and it's beautiful. "Thank you. I like you guys too. I really do."

"Goodness sake, don't cry." Tessa passes me a napkin. "We didn't tell you that to upset you."

"I know," I say. "I just . . ."

"You've been through a lot," finishes Clem for me.

"After that woman turning up at work the other day, I'm not really surprised you're a bit emotional." Tessa tosses her hair. I wish I were that cool. "But it's okay, Anna. Things are going to get better for you."

"I believe that," I say. "I do."

"Good."

"You've come a long way," says Clem with a gentle smile. She's been there too. Having to rebuild her existence from the ground up.

"I'm happy with how things are going." And it's the truth. "Thank you for hanging out with me today and getting me over my idiocy."

"I'm still not completely convinced it's idiocy," says Clem.

"No. It is. I'm too old for this unrequited bullshit. I should know better."

"You're single and human." Clem picks up a French fry and waves it about with much meaning. "You're still breathing. Why shouldn't you have many and varied hopes and dreams?"

"Hmm."

"You mean because of the divorce?" asks Tessa.

I nod. "There should be a compulsory waiting period before

you can get all attached and lusty after a major breakup. A deep cleansing period. Like an enema for the emotions."

Clem laughs. "That doesn't sound extreme at all."

"I repeat, the heart is not sensible," says Tessa.

"But maybe you can train it to be." I ponder the thought. "I have a plan. I'm going to avoid him for a few days until I've got myself back under control, then carry on as if this never happened."

Tessa just stares. "That's your plan, huh?"

"Yep."

"Does denial and avoidance really work, though?" asks Clem.

"Not even a little." Tessa steals a fry. "But best of luck to you, girl."

I smile. "Thank you."

It's around midnight when I sneak into the condo. Mom and Dad were surprised but happy to see me. Dad even managed to make conversation with me regarding subjects other than the sad demise of my marriage to his best buddy Ryan. And thank God for that. I also spent quality time talking to Briar and dissecting her new relationship with a hot dude who tends bar at her favorite club. All in all, a highly successful day out and about. A day that largely did not involve Leif. Go, me.

The condo is in darkness, everything quiet. I don't turn on a light and I don't make a sound. Mostly. Leif and his lady friend are probably in bed. Or maybe they're out partying. Living their best lives. Who knows? Not me. Either way, I'm getting to bed without any more weird confrontations. And anyway, it doesn't even matter. That's the truth of things. I have made peace with my situation. We're friends and that's all. My confused heart can just stop making bad choices. I am moving on with my life.

I slip off my flats at the door and feel my way carefully forward. The night is so still I can hear the soft hum of music coming from one of our neighbors upstairs. Something bluesy. From the window comes the faint glow of streetlights and there's the shadow of a tree limb shifting gently on the wall. Truth is, I could have been a super spy. A secret agent or something. My careful quiet progress into the condo is going so damn well. My hand is extended, reaching for the back of the couch, which absolutely has to be there. Or at least very close. Only my hand is too high and I find it care of my bare foot slamming into the couch foot with much damn oomph.

"Fuck," I gasp.

Pain shoots up my leg and holy hell. This hurts. One of the overhead lights turns on and there is Leif, leaning against the wall in the opening of the hallway. He does not look amused. Given I'm the one who almost just broke a toe, I have no idea what he's got to be grumpy about.

I hop around to the other side of the couch and sit down. Oh my poor, innocent pinkie toe. I feel so bad for me. "Shit, shit, shit. Did I wake you?"

"No," he says, crossing his arms. "I couldn't sleep."

My stomach drops. "Did you have a nightmare?"

"I was waiting up for you."

"Oh."

With a sigh, he heads for the fridge, making up an impromptu ice pack with a kitchen towel and a bundle of the cold stuff for me. The sound of the ice hitting the countertop is startlingly loud in the silence. Then he kneels at my feet, frowning at my injury. Carefully, the ice pack is held against my wounded toe. He's in his sleep pants again. No tee. Far too much skin for my peace of mind. There's no call for him to be flaunting his nipples and pecs in the privacy of his own home. Talk about disgusting.

"Why didn't you just turn on a light when you came in?" he asks.

"I was trying not to disturb you. Did you have a nice day with your friend?" I ask, playing it cool. All puns intended.

"We had lunch," he says.

"Mm."

Therein follows a couple of awkward moments wherein he stares at my foot and I stare at anything that isn't him. Or at least try to. My fascination with the man is hard to figure. Rational thought dictates that I should be burnt out from my divorce and in need/want of time and space. And yet the one thing I feel like I might actually need/want is him. Which is terrifying. The timing of this crush is just awful in all the ways. But grown-ass women can control their emotions and behavior. At least I hope I can.

"Why were you waiting up for me?" I ask at last.

"Things felt off this morning." His voice is low and gravelly. "Thought we could talk about it."

"What?" I scoff. "No."

His brow goes up. "Is that you denying things were weird, or refusing to discuss them with me?"

"Both." It's out of my mouth before I can stop it. Dammit.

"Anna." He shakes his head. "I thought we were past this."

"Past what?"

"You running away when things get tough," he says, resting back on his haunches. "Trust and understanding, remember?"

I have nothing.

"Bestie, buddy, roommate . . ."

At this, I flinch. I can't help it. The R word is killing me. I'm the worst friend ever.

"Okay," he says. As if something's been decided. "Thing is, I didn't know Roshuane was stopping by and I—"

"You're allowed to have people over whenever you want. It's none of my business."

"Let me finish," he says, taking a deep breath. "We used to be involved, but things are different now. My interests currently lie elsewhere. So we went and had a nice lunch and we're probably going to catch up in a couple of weeks' time for a drink or something. That's it."

And I sit there frozen. "That's your private business. You didn't need to tell me all that."

"Do you feel better for me having told you all that?"

"Yes," I admit.

"There you go then." With another sigh, he sets the ice pack aside and joins me on the sofa. "I think you need to do the thing we talked about you doing a while back."

I draw my brows together. "What? What thing?"

"You know."

"No, I don't know."

Yet another sigh. Never has a man been more put upon. Just ask him. "How's your toe?"

"Sore."

"You think it might be broken? Want me to take you to a medical center to get it checked?"

I think it over, carefully moving the appendage. "No. It's probably just a sprain or something. I don't think there's much they can do about toes. I'll see how it is tomorrow."

"Okay." He nods. "Let me know if you change your mind."

"Do you want me to move out?" I ask, dreading the answer.

"What? No. Of course not."

My shoulders slump. "Oh."

He shakes his head, a half smile curling one corner of his lips. "Anna. Baby. At least I'll never have to wonder what you're thinking. It's all written right there on your face. You're the least mysterious woman I've ever met."

"I am too mysterious."

"No," he says in a definitive voice. "And I can't tell you what a fucking relief that is. Every woman I've ever known has pretty much had me in a constant state of confusion. But not you."

"I'm not sure this is a compliment."

"With you, it's more like a semi-constant state." He tucks his hands behind his head and relaxes back against them. "A now-and-then sort of thing instead of an endless everyday 'what the fuck does she mean and why the hell is she mad at me now?' I actually have a fighting chance at figuring shit out with you. It's a hell of a thing."

"You're rambling. What were we talking about before?"

"I was referring to that time you hit on me."

I freeze.

"You remember."

Give me strength. "I could hardly forget."

"Don't be embarrassed," he says, as if it makes everything better. "You were drunk and horny and dealing with a lot. Like, more than most people ever have to deal with in a lifetime. I thought you did quite well keeping your shit together."

"Thanks," I say drily.

"We all makes mistakes now and then."

"Great."

"And if we'd gotten involved then, it would have been a mistake." He stares off at nothing, pondering this for a moment. "A *big* mistake."

I slide down. I'd disappear if I could. "Right."

"Huge, even."

"You're doing absolutely nothing for my ego."

"Huh? Oh. Hang in there." He pats me on the knee and then goes so far as to leave his hand there lingering for a moment. "The point I'm trying to make, Anna, is that that was then and this is now."

"So?"

"So you should try again," he announces with a smile.

"What?"

"Try again," he encourages. "Come on to me."

I wrinkle my nose in his general direction. He cannot be saying what I think he's saying. Impossible.

"I told you at the time if you were still interested to proposition me again in a couple of months," he says, holding his palms out in front of him. "Here we are. Why not give it a go?"

"Because you rejected me?"

"Yeah, but I explained that."

"Leif," I say, pausing to take a breath. "You're offering yourself up here like some game of chance. The only thing is, when I lose at this game it's not only humiliating, but it hurts."

"Anna." His gaze softens. Something about the way he says

my name turns me into goo. This man . . . holy hell. "We didn't talk about it before you tried to kiss me last time so there wasn't much I could do. But this time, we've already got all of our talking out of the way. Do you really think I'd set you up to fail?"

I don't know what to say. He's dead serious. And all of a sudden my heart is hammering inside my chest.

"The look on your face this morning killed me," he says. "But there was no way I was ever going to restart something with Roshuane while there's something happening between me and you."

"You're interested in me?" And I sound so small and fragile. I hate it, but I can't help it.

"Have I not been chasing your gorgeous ass around for months now?"

I frown. "Have you?"

His brows rise. "Well, I have for me."

"Huh."

"Are you coming over here or what?" he asks. "I feel like we need to hug it out. And stuff."

"And stuff?"

He tips his chin. "C'mon, Anna. Take a chance. I won't let you fall."

Never has covering a couple of feet worth of couch been so fraught with danger. So loaded with meaning. Not that I have any real clue what any of this means. Nor am I going to stop to think about it right now. I can overthink things later at my leisure. Right now, I'm a great big freaked-out ball of nerves with a throbbing toe. A hug from Leif sounds wonderful. I no sooner rise up on one knee than he's grabbed me by the waist and dragged me onto his lap. Only we're chest to chest this time.

I'm sitting straddling his body and what a body it is. His arms wrap around me and I rest my cheek on his shoulder. My breasts press against his firm chest and I'm not going to cry because that would be weird. It just feels like coming home. It's also just been a big day. A big couple of days. A big year.

"This is better," he says, letting out a deep breath.

"Yeah."

So much bare skin it's going to my head. If only I could will my tee and bra out of existence so that there's nothing between us. That would be sublime. He's so big and brawny and beautiful with his muscles and tattoos. With the way he's so totally at ease with himself. Meanwhile, I'm not sure where to put my hands first. Where I'm allowed to touch and what I'm allowed do now that the rules between us are changing so fast.

His head rests against mine and we just cling to each other for a moment. A long moment. I'd crawl under his skin and make myself at home if I could. After all of the uncertainty, it's good to be this close. Like we're melting into each other. Like nothing could ever come between us. This hug is everything. Right up until I feel his fingers creeping under the hem of my tee and up my back. The rough skin on the pad of his thumb rubbing back and forth across my skin gives me goose bumps. All of the little hairs on the back of my neck stand on end. The man is electric.

"I thought I was meant to be making the move," I mumble.

"You took too long." He rubs his nose against my hair, even pausing to sniff. Whatever turns him on. "Figured you needed some encouragement."

Which is about when his fingers reverse direction and dip below the back of my jeans to trace the waistband of my panties. Plain sensible white cotton, but you can't have everything.

What's really nice, or indeed, exciting, about all of this is the feel of him starting to harden against me. Someone other than my ex wants to sleep with me and the accident hasn't stolen my feminine allure. My elusive girl power. Amazing. Two stupid concerns crossed off the list. This is all doing my confidence untold amounts of good.

"You'll tell me if you're uncomfortable or anything?" he asks.

"Mm-hmm."

"Your toe's okay?" he continues. "Your muscles aren't cramping or sore?"

"All good."

With one hand wrapped around the back of his neck in case he tries to escape or something, I nuzzle my way up to his ear. What a thing of pleasure he is. There's a musky male scent to him that's high inducing. Since he's made no attempts to throw me off, I let go of my hold on his neck and experiment with running my fingers over his stubble. Then there's the thickness of his shoulders and the swell of his pecs, his sensitive flat nipples all just waiting to be caressed. I could pet him for hours. And I just might.

Meanwhile, his fingers are gripping the tops of my ass cheeks, encouraging me to press against him. Encouraging me to grind myself against him. I haven't been this close to anyone in a long time and it's a dizzying good thing.

He turns his head, his lips pressing against my forehead. Such a sweet man. "I usually have more control than this."

"It's fine."

I thread my hands through his hair, testing the silken strands. He's a dichotomy of sensations. Soft hair and hard muscles. Rough stubble and smooth lips. I rub my thumb over his bottom lip and he fakes taking a bite. This time at least. The heat in his gaze makes me think he enjoys this sort of thing. Playing a little rough. Sounds like fun to me.

"You okay?" he asks.

"I'm good."

"You're sure?"

"Yes." Good and sure along with a little annoyed now, actually. "Am I doing anything to make you think otherwise?"

"No, I just—"

"I'm not fragile, Leif. You're not going to accidentally break me or something."

He just blinks. "Well, baby, to be honest . . . I'd bend you over the nearest table and fuck you hard except I was trying to take shit slow and be romantic since this is our first time and all. Maybe you just want a make-out session and that's fine with me. I'm happy just to have my hands on you, so it's your call."

"That so?"

"Yep."

Which is about when I grab his gorgeous face and kiss him like my life depends on it. Because in that moment it sort of does. I am not a mess. I am neither a patient nor a problem. Hell no. I am the woman who is going to shake him up some. Strong arms band around me, holding on tight, while our mouths fight for dominance. My tongue tangles with his and I take his breath into me. He tastes of toothpaste and hot man. And Leif doesn't hold back in the least.

Any curiosity regarding the size of his dick is also fast being sated. There's no doubting the heat and hardness pressing into me. Sleeping pants don't leave much to the imagination, bless them.

Hair mussed by my hands and lips swollen by our kiss, he damn near takes my breath away with his beauty. I want to write him bad poetry and hang his picture on my bedroom wall. Do all of the things with him and for him. It's scary to feel so much so fast.

"I want to say something clever and charming, but I've got nothing," he says as his mouth grazes along my jawline.

"No?"

"You're real pretty," he murmurs in a rough voice.

"Thank you. So are you."

Everything low in my belly is honed in on the feel of him against me. The way we fit together just so. My panties are wet, my pussy swollen. And we've barely gotten started. At some stage, he's slipped a hand up the front of my shirt. I don't recall when. Clever fingers ease my bra cup out of the way. He takes one breast in hand, squeezing and kneading it just so, rubbing his thumb back and forth across the hardening nipple. His other hand rests against my spine, keeping me close, urging me to keep rocking.

This time when he kisses me it's slow and sure. Teeth nibble on my bottom lip. His tongue flicks against mine with expert precision. It's deep and thorough, as if he's learning me. Seducing me even. The happy humming noise he makes sends a thrill straight through me. I trail my hands down his chest, through his scattering of chest hair, over the start of his six-pack, and then over to his sides. Which is where his shoulders hitch up and he stops me with a gasp.

"Don't," he says.

"What?"

Nothing from him. But he grips my hands and relocates

them to higher ground. Back up on his pecs. The smile he gives me is odd, to say the least.

"I can't touch you down there?" I ask with a frown. Which is when it occurs to me. "Wait. Are you ticklish?"

"Only a little."

"On your sides?"

A grunt. "Some."

"That's so cute."

"It's manly," he corrects.

"Sure. That too."

As my fingers start to trail downward again he snaps, "Don't do it."

"I'm not doing anything."

"You forget," he says, wrapping my arms around his neck. "You are not mysterious. I can read you like a book."

"That's harsh."

"Okay. You're a little mysterious. But you're still not tickling me." He licks his damp lips. "Otherwise, I'll be forced to interrupt proceedings by throwing your fine ass on the bed and conducting vile and twisted experiments to discover your own ticklish spots."

"Oh."

"Yeah. Oh."

"I don't like being tickled," I say.

"Then let me suggest an alternative course of events."

"I'm listening."

He grabs the hem of my tee, carefully tugging it up and over my head. My bra is as wonky as can be, with one boob proudly on display care of his earlier ministrations. Not a good look.

Fortunately for all, Leif has the undergarment gone in no time at all. A useful guy to have around.

"Okay. Here's the plan," he says with all due seriousness. Next he stands, taking me with him on account of my arms and legs now being wrapped around him. But we don't go far. Only into my bedroom, where I'm deposited on the mattress. He then divests me of jeans and panties. I'm now officially bare-ass naked. For a second, it's tempting to try and cover up. Ultimately, however, this would be a stupid move. And my various scars and assorted wobbly or dimpled bits don't seem to bother him. Confidence in all things. Or at least a solid attempt at same.

"This is the plan?" I ask.

"You naked on your bed. That is the whole plan. What do you think?"

"I propose an amendment to the plan." I nod. "Lose your pants."

"Not yet."

I'm on the verge of whining in a ladylike manner when he drops to his knees at the side of the bed, grabs my legs, and tugs me toward the edge of the mattress.

Okay then.

All of my dimpled and wobbly bits are on display and there's no opportunity for me to cover myself or try to hide. Nor should I need to. Time to grow up and get confident. We're doing this right now. Obviously he's okay with my body, however, because next my legs are draped over his shoulders. Without further ado the man plants his face in my pussy. And then he says something. Something I cannot decipher, though it sends a thrill straight through me on account of his positioning.

"What?" I ask, smiling. I can't help it. His lips moving

against my labia, his breath against all of that oversensitive flesh. Maybe he's a pussy whisperer. Who knows?

"You smell good," he says before dragging his tongue through me. My back bows and holy hell. The rough of his stubble down there carefully grazing against me is amazing. So facial hair does have a useful application after all. "And you taste even better."

There's no time for me to respond. No space in my brain for formulating words. Not with the way he holds my sex open with his thumbs and gets busy eating me. It's more enthusiasm than anything. His tongue licking and teeth nibbling. The suction and sheer overwhelming dedication to the task. I've never had a man come at me with such eagerness. In no time at all, the heat is building, the pressure mounting, and I'm grinding my ass into the bed. Not sure if I want to get away or get more. Most likely the latter. It's just a lot.

I haven't felt so much in . . . pretty much forever.

The lower half of my body is ignited. The rush of it spilling out over me from top to toe. When he sucks on my clit, toying with it with his tongue, I'm done for. Dead. Deceased. With a choked whimper it crashes over me, claiming me, and I'm just the remains of a woman left lying on the bed.

It takes a while for my thighs to stop shaking. In that time, Leif has taken a swig from the water bottle on my bedside table and stands considering me. "It's been a while for you, huh?"

I nod.

"Me too."

Without a word, I crawl further onto the mattress, taking a moment to pull myself together. To wonder what comes next.

The expression on his face is distant. Contemplative. "Once isn't going to be enough. Is that all right with you?"

"Shouldn't we see if we're any good together before making any ongoing commitments?"

His smile is sneaky. Amused. "You really think we're going to be lacking in chemistry? After that performance?"

It's hard to talk to a man with a dick pointing toward the ceiling. Hard to keep your eyes on his face, at any rate. Dicks are distracting. Or his is. Noting the object my gaze is drawn to, he slips his thumbs beneath the waistband of his sleeping pants and drops them to the ground. Yes. That's definitely an engorged penis. My guess was right. And he's thick and long and all things good and right and then some. His penis is a thing of beauty.

Thank you, Baby Jesus.

"You got condoms in here?" he asks.

"Bedside drawer."

He retrieves the unopened box and sorts out the prophylactic requirements in no time. I can't help watch him, spellbound by his every movement. By his naked body. By his big hands moving in sure and swift movements. Then he crawls onto the bed toward me, situating himself between my legs.

"My fine lady," he says in a low voice. "I am doth here to prove myself. And my fine appendage."

"I don't think that's how you use that word."

"Appendage?"

"Doth."

"Ah."

And he covers me with the heat of his body, his weight taken by one elbow situated beside my head. My world is suddenly small and intimate and smells damn good. I don't know what to do with my hands. With any of me, actually. This is all so good, but strange at the same time.

"Why are you nervous?" he asks, kissing along my jawline.

"I don't know."

"No?"

"No," I lie.

It hasn't been a year for good things. I've gotten scarily used to disappointment. While the odds of this here between us not working out are minimal, I don't want to get my hopes up just the same. Just in case. But it's hard to keep your expectations under control when there's a smokin' hot man in your bed. When he's decided to make you his sole focus. Then there's the worries in the back of my head. Stupid things like, where does this leave us now that we've exposed our genitals to each other? Stuff like that.

One of his hands trails down my torso, pausing to plump my breast, and there's no room left for thinking. Next his mouth is there, his lips sucking. It's fucking exquisite. And the heat in his eyes. The darkness of his gaze. It's all so honest and hungry and perfect.

"It's okay, Anna," he says, moving his mouth back to my lips. "It's just us."

"Yeah."

"Just you and me."

He positions the hard, wide head of his cock at my entrance and starts pushing in. Oh so slowly. Next he grips my thigh, encouraging me to wrap him up in my legs. That I can do. My body tenses slightly, taking a moment to adapt to his presence inside of me. It really has been a while. But it feels so good, him stretching me, taking me. So solid and substantial.

His hips work against me and he sinks deeper and deeper. I know I've got all of him when he squeezes his eyelids shut, resting his forehead against mine.

"Give me a minute," he says.

His hair forms a curtain around us and I can handle this better. Knowing that I'm affecting him too. That it's been a while for him too. I stroke his arms and his shoulders. There's a light sheen of sweat on his skin already. His neck is so thick. Never knew I was into thick necks before, but here we are. Because every inch of this man works for me. My thighs tighten on his hips and I guess my insides tighten on him well because he hisses and presses a hard, swift kiss to my mouth.

"Shit. Baby. You feel amazing," he says, just making conversation. "I knew you would."

"You thought about that?"

"All the fucking time." He opens his eyes, staring down at me with a smile. "You comfortable? All good?"

"Yes and yes."

"Excellent. Well, I'd be delighted to say all sorts of sweet and smutty things to you later. But right now I have things to do. Like you," he specifies. "You're the thing I have to do."

"Got it."

And he draws back before pushing back into me good and hard. I'm wet and wanting. I can take it. But it steals the breath from me just the same. There's definitely no more time for talking. Fucking is the priority. Because there's no way this is making love. This is hot and sweaty and fast and hard. His muscles flex and his face sharpens and all I can do is hang on for the ride. And the ride is spectacular. He is magic. He sets a determined pace, undoing me piece by piece until I'm one big ball of need. Nothing beyond this bed exists.

The focus on his face and set of his jawline is mesmerizing. He strokes me deep inside, lighting me up, building that high all over again. A normally impossible feat for me, but nothing is impossible when it comes to Leif. His hips grind against me, driving me into a frenzy. The base of his cock rubbing against my clit in a way that is honestly stellar. And when he finds a particularly thrilling spot and works it over and over again, raw electricity streaks up and down my spine. It's like he knows my body better than I do and isn't the least bit hesitant to show me.

His hand closes over my throat just firmly enough to make its presence known and his voice is guttural as he says, "Look at me."

I can do nothing else as the whole world bleeds to gray and my body seizes. Waves of pleasure swamp me. There's just him. Just him and me. And he's all I've got to hold onto.

Leif curses and comes, slamming his hips against me.

We're a hot wet mess on the mattress. His face in my neck, his back heaving as he sucks in air. I well know the feeling. Mostly, I'm limp. Floppy. Spent. Words like that. If we never moved again it would be fine with me. But oh so carefully, he disentangles himself and collapses beside me on the mattress. Probably for the best. As much as I like the feel of his weight pressing me down, the man is heavy. I smell like him. Hell, I'm covered in him and it's wonderful. The man shook me up good and proper, then delivered on heaven. Easily the best sex I've ever had. How about that?

The quiet unnerves me. Or maybe it's the sense of peace and contentment. I don't trust it. "Are you okay?"

"Shh," he says, eyelids sealed shut. "Post-come float."

Huh.

For a long time, nothing is said. Then finally he comes out with, "Not bad for a first effort."

I just look at him and blink. "Not bad?"

He frowns. "What? You didn't like it?"

That's when I hide my head under a pillow. This man's going to be the death of me.

CHAPTER SEVEN

"**S**TOP IT."

"Hmm?" I look up from my bowl of chocolate cake and ice cream. Sex and baking is apparently now our life. Good times.

"You're thinking a lot and not saying anything," he says, pointing his spoon at me in an accusatory fashion. He's sitting cross-legged opposite me on the bed. The only thing he's wearing is a fetching navy-and-white-striped apron. I at least put on a tee and panties. Talk about decorum. His hair is tied back and his expression is so open and honest. "Also, you're licking the spoon in a gratuitous manner."

"Am not. You just have a dirty mind."

"Anna, tell me what you're thinking."

"It's nothing really."

"C'mon, humor me," he says. Then pauses. "Wait. Let me guess. You're thinking about the ex, right?"

I shrug.

"I knew it. Do you feel guilty?"

"No. A little strange maybe, but not guilty."

"Strange in what way?" he asks, cocking his head.

"I don't mean to compare, but I can't help comparing sometimes," I admit.

"Go on."

I wince. "Lief . . ."

"C'mon. It's okay. Whatever you have to say, I can handle it." His smile is gentle, cautious. "But I don't want you bottling shit up and stressing over things. I know you're an overthinker, but we need to set limits for everyone's sake. Get it off your chest, Anna. I am your therapist. With sexual benefits."

"Is that what we are now?" I ask, beyond curious. "Roommates with benefits?"

"You need a label?"

"Yeah. I think I do."

"Okay." He sighs. "Truth is, I don't know. I like you and I assume you like me."

"You're not so bad."

"Thanks," he says. "I especially like you naked in bed and am more than happy to return the favor for you if you're in agreement."

"The fact that we're sitting scantily clad on my bed would suggest I'm good with that."

"Right." He nods. "So I say we add sex-friend to the roommate title and see where that gets us for now. What do you say?"

"Sure."

"Now tell me what you're thinking about. It's good to share. And you know you're safe with me."

Guess he has a point. Sharing in any kind of relationship is necessary. It's quite possibly one of the areas where I let the team down in the last one. Because despite the divorce not being my fault, I can definitely do better in the future. I hope. So I sit up straighter, pulling myself together. "I knew it would be different having sex with someone else, it just kind of surprised me is all."

"In what way?"

"I don't know . . . it's hard to describe exactly. And some of it kind of sucks to own up to," I admit. "Like, I might have been married to Ryan, but in a lot of ways I'm more open with you."

"It wasn't the thing I did with my . . ." He wriggles his pinkie finger. That finger had done things to me. Rude things.

"No. Though that was a little surprising."

"You'll tell me if there's anything you don't want me to do, right?" he asks.

"Right," I say. "But I wasn't talking about physically so much as emotionally. Which is odd considering we're not exactly in a relationship."

"Eh. We sort of are."

"We just agreed to be roommates with benefits."

He raises a brow. "That's not a relationship?"

"Not really. Not in the way most people would think of a romantic relationship partnership sort of thing."

"Good God, this is complicated," he says. "No wonder I steer clear of this shit normally. Can't we just enjoy being together? Hanging out?"

"We can do that. We *are* doing that."

"Phew. All right then."

I give him my practiced polite smile. Only he's too busy contemplating his chocolate cake to notice.

"You think maybe you trust me more than you trusted him?" he asks eventually after swirling the frosting around on his bowl with his spoon for a while. "Or do you think the accident and subsequent bullshit sort of broke you down and opened you up a little?"

"I honestly don't know."

"It was a hell of a thing to go through. It wouldn't be surprising if your view of the world and your place in it had undergone some changes."

"Is that what happened with your accident and . . . everything else?" I don't want to bring up the ex who used and abused him and tried to kill Clem. But it is relevant to the topic of conversation.

He thinks it over for a moment. "I was bitter for a long time. Maybe I still am a bit. It made it hard to trust people, you know?"

"Yeah."

"But I'm getting there," he says. "How about you?"

"I hope I'm getting there. It hasn't really been that long. Makes it kind of hard to say."

"Hmm."

"Guess I'll have to think about it."

"I'm sure you will," he says with all due seriousness. "In the meantime, how do you feel about me smearing chocolate frosting on your tits and licking it off?"

"Sounds messy."

"But fun, right?"

And the dude is grinning like it's Christmas. How could I possibly say no?

Monday is spent having sex, watching movies, and doing laundry. Frosting and body fluids are a sticky combination. We watch more *Twilight* because *Twilight*, the eternal battle between

Edward's poetically floppy hair and Jacob's muscles, must go on. Leif also talks me into watching an awesome Indonesian action-thriller called *The Raid*. Food-wise, our lessons in the kitchen include making pasta carbonara from scratch since I got the pasta machine in the divorce. This was also an excellent excuse to open a bottle of Pinot Grigio.

A very good day off is had by all. Tuesday and the work-week returns all too soon.

"A sternum tattoo?" I ask with a smile that's as fake as can be. "Wow."

"I'm ready for you, Courtney," says Leif, standing by the back hallway. Because the room out back is necessary for work requiring some privacy due to the exposure of certain body parts. Like breasts.

Courtney is a perky blonde. I shouldn't have used the word *perky*. Poor choice.

My roommate with benefits flashes me a smile before disappearing into said room with the girl. Woman. Client.

Meanwhile, Ed is watching me with a speculative gaze while he sips his coffee. His first appointment for the day cancelled due to illness. Though Ed doesn't seem particularly upset or anything by the loss of work. Guess there are always other jobs to do when you own a small business.

He too receives my best fake smile.

"She'll be wearing tape over her nipples if it makes it any better," he says in a quiet voice.

So I really am an open book. "Not particularly."

"It's just part of the job, Anna."

"I know. It's fine, really."

He does not appear convinced. "Doctors have to look at body bits all day long, too."

I nod. Because he isn't telling me anything I don't know. I just don't particularly like it. That's the truth of the situation. "You're not concerned about us being involved and working together?"

He just shrugs.

"Okay."

"You know, I asked him if he wanted a couple of tickets to a band that was passing through town last night. A friend of ours had bought them, then couldn't make it," says Ed, all in the same quiet reasonable tone. "I happen to know my brother loves that band. He only missed out on buying tickets because they sold out too damn fast."

"Huh."

"You know what he told me?"

"What?"

"He said he had to stay home and wash his hair."

I snort. What a clown. We did in fact have sex in the shower, so it wasn't entirely a lie. But he'd also known that crowds and loud noises tend to wear on me. Standing up for long periods of time isn't great either. While I might have gone if he asked, it would have worn me out and we have work today.

"Then he waltzes in here this morning with a stupid grin on his face," continues Ed. "My brother is not a morning person. Smiles before midday are in limited supply. But not today."

I keep my mouth shut.

"The little shit is practically walking on sunshine."

"The little shit is over thirty years old and more than six feet tall."

His serious façade cracks for a moment. "Yeah. But he's always going to be my little brother."

I smile.

"We came out big," he says. "All three of us were up around ten pounds. Mom still bitches about giving birth naturally."

"Ouch."

"Clem says if we ever go there she's taking every drug on offer."

"And I do not blame her one iota."

He smiles.

I cross my arms. A purely defensive position given where I'm about to take the conversation. "Thought for sure you'd have some concerns about us getting involved."

"You're adults. If you think you can live and work together and still manage a relationship then that's on you two," he says, taking another sip of coffee. "I trust you both not to bring any shit in here. To behave professionally and so on."

I nod. "We're not really in a relationship, though. Exactly. It's, um, it's something else."

He just looks at me.

Oh my God. Talk about overshare. My mouth needs to stay shut.

"It's complicated, huh?" he asks with a gentle smile.

"Yeah."

"I've been meaning to thank you, actually." He takes a seat on one of the stools on wheels we have around the place. "Leif hasn't been himself the last year or so. What with everything that happened. You've brought him back to life in a lot of ways."

"Oh." And that's all I've got. Go, conversation skills.

"He trusts you. I mean, he's spending less time on his own,

going out more, doing stuff," he says. "Things were pretty grim there for a while, so it's really good to see."

"I'm glad."

"He was just . . . down on everything. Especially after all the shit that happened." A trace of fury crosses his face. Along with something close to guilt. "It was kind of a shock to see him that way. He's always been the joker, you know? The positive person that makes everyone laugh and never takes anything seriously. Sometimes to his detriment. But it's like his heart was full of hate there for a while. Everything weighed him down. The accident, that the police couldn't find the guy, then there was the amount of pain he was in with his arm all fucked up. You helped shift the remnants of all that and I'm grateful."

"He's a good friend," I say. Because what the hell am I supposed to say?

"Clem said your divorce was finalized on Friday."

"Yes."

"Must be a weight off your mind."

"It really is."

This is the part where some people would warn me to maybe not get involved with their little brother, what with how my own life has been so riddled with strife lately. Suggest I take some time to get my own shit together. But Ed doesn't do that. Which I appreciate.

"I better get started on these sketches," he says instead, picking up his tablet. "Try not to worry about what he's doing. Because I assure you, he's not getting up to anything. Tattooing takes focus and concentration. One moment of distraction is one moment too many."

"Mm."

He frowns. "You're a worrier. You're going to worry anyway."

"Yeah."

There's nothing much more to say. We both go back to our own work. It was a nice chat, all in all. My new boss is a nice guy. Leif is lucky to be surrounded by people who care about him. Not that I'm a lonely girl or anything. We're both lucky.

I get back to updating the books on the laptop sitting on the front shop counter. Things are looking good. I've also been doing some research into conventions Ed and co might want to consider attending, along with other possible avenues of promotion. Though it seems to work mostly on word of mouth in this industry. Social media has a role to play. There's also a new line of inks they might want to take a look at. I've been organizing some samples for the shop.

Yep. Lots to think about. Plenty to do.

And the thing with a sternum tattoo is that you're not just going to see bare breasts, but there's a very strong chance you'll be touching them too. I mean, you'd have to. Lift them up. Hold them out of the way. Maneuver them here and there. Things like that. With gloves on, but still. The fact remains that my special sexual someone is perhaps right now handling another woman's breasts. I must have feelings about this. Lots of feelings. My mind, however, is a mess. I'm having issues sorting out exactly what those feelings might be.

Stupid thing is, I didn't have the presence of mind to ask if we were exclusive. I mean, I think we are. Probably. I'd be highly impressed with his organizational skills if he did manage to find time to see another woman given all of the time we spend together. All right, so I wouldn't be impressed, I'd be pissed. Are we together? I wouldn't say that exactly. Together kind of entails a commitment of some description. Are we dating then? Sort of? No, we're not. Because that would entail going out on dates and we're not doing that. We just added sex to our regular hanging-out activities. And hey, I'm not complaining. The sex is amazing. Best I've ever had. Guess I just have questions. Like what are the rules in this situation?

But it's his job. It's just his job.

He did not ask for that woman to take her top off. And if he walks out of the back office and I'm immediately all up in his face with my insecurities it won't be good. I need to be cool about this. Bring it up all casual like later when we're at home. Just sort of have a chat about things. Again.

God knows how long I've been staring off at nothing contemplating Leif's hands on another woman's body, but Courtney comes out of the back room, still tugging on her loose top. I jump to my feet for some reason. Not on edge at all.

"Time for a cigarette," she says.

I fake smile again because customer service matters. Also, my boobs are a bit smaller than hers and about five years older. That's five extra years of dealing with gravity and underwire, thank you very much. Oh well. There's nothing I can do about them right here and now. Not that I would if I could. Heck. I'm driving myself insane.

Behind her comes Leif, looking no different regardless of where his hands have been. Jeans, sneakers, and a tee featuring Godzilla. He'd suggested this morning that it was a subtle reference to his monster-size dick. Bless him. He keeps right on walking until he's backed me against the counter.

"Hi," he says.

"Hi."

Our faces are close and our bodies even closer.

"I guess we're not playing it cool at work?" I ask. Another thing we forgot to talk about.

"Eh. Whatever." He gives his brother a disinterested glance over his shoulder. "Unless you want me to play it cool at work? You're not worried about idiot over there, are you?"

Ed calmly raises his middle finger and keeps setting up for his next client.

"You mean my boss?" I ask.

"Yeah. Him."

"I guess not," I say. "I mean, he seems okay with us."

"Of course he is."

"Though this does seem a little beyond roommates with benefits."

He scratches at his stubble. "You think?"

"What I think is that we should talk later."

Leif blinks. "You want to talk?"

"Yes."

"Okay." He shifts even closer. "I don't have a lunch break today, so can it wait until we go home?"

"Yes."

"So we'll go home, talk about whatever you want to talk about, and then I'll dance for you."

My brows rise. "You're going to dance for me?"

"Yes, I am."

Ed snorts. He tries to turn it into a cough, but it's not very believable.

"Did you study dance when you were at school or something?" I ask, curious. Honestly, nothing would surprise me when it comes to Leif.

But it's Ed that answers, "He was on the cheer team for like three weeks because he thought it'd get him in with the hot girls. But all that happened was he pulled a hamstring showing off trying to do a backflip."

I bite back a smile.

"I wasn't trying to do a backflip," says Leif. "I was executing one perfectly. Right up until the hamstring went ping. My dream career cut tragically short."

"That's so sad." Still trying not to smile. "I feel bad for you."

"Thanks." He inspects my forehead. "Anna, you're 'I'm worried' line is on display."

"My 'I'm worried' line?"

He tips his chin. "When you're overthinking something with all your heart and soul, you get a little line between your eyebrows. It's how I know to tread carefully."

"I'm really not mysterious."

"You're really not," he agrees. "But I like you anyway. Can you give me a hint what's going on?"

I sigh. I even make me tired sometimes. "It's okay, really. Like you said, I'm just overthinking things. We'll talk about it later."

"If you say so." He's not happy. "Later, then."

The bell above the door rings as Courtney steps back inside. She smiles, but she's not looking quite as perky as before. Her movements are careful, and there's a tightness about her eyes and jaw. She doesn't look like someone enthusing about baring her perfect breasts to a hot stranger. More like someone willing herself to push through the pain and get through this. Getting your sternum tattooed might not be quite as sexy as I'd been imagining.

Then Leif smacks his mouth against mine, kissing me hard

and fast. It's hot and frenzied and has quite the impact. And he doesn't go light on the tongue. The kiss leaves absolutely no doubt in anyone's mind as to who he's with. As statements go, it's a pretty great one.

"You good for now?" he asks.

"I'm good for now."

Then he nods.

I'm still smiling, dazed and confused, when Leif and Courtney disappear out back once more. It doesn't matter whose body parts he'd fondling on behalf of his job. The man is with me.

Ed shakes his head. "Told you."

"You told me," I agree. "Do you really think he's going to dance for me?"

"Just don't let him try the backflip."

"I always thought you were way too tense for someone who was apparently getting it on the regular," says Briar over FaceTime.

"Really?"

"Oh, yeah."

We've already dissected a TV series, a handbag I'm thinking of buying, and certain passive-aggressive tendencies displayed by a new barista at Briar's favorite coffee shop. Girl talk for the win.

"Huh," I say. "It never occurred to me that my sex life with the Ex affected my demeanor, but who knows?"

"It's a known fact that when the orgasms are good you're in a better mood."

"This does make sense."

"Ryan was a nice enough guy up to a point," she says. "But

I had my reservations as to whether he was capable of actually getting the job done."

"You thought about my ex and me having sex?" I ask, trying not to laugh. "Ew."

She laughs too. "Like we haven't dissected my sex life constantly over the past not quite a decade. God, you can be a big baby. I considered the physical satisfaction and welfare of my friend. It basically makes me a good person. And don't act like you're incapable of being an inappropriate gossip queen when it suits you. I know you too well for this."

"This is true." I sigh. "This revelation fascinates me. What the hell gave it away?"

"He's just one of those men that have issues seeing beyond themselves, I think. Women are like an adjunct to them. As if we're not quite real on some level. Like our wants and needs are lesser somehow. And if they're not seeing us as people, then why take the time and trouble to see to our bedroom needs beyond the basic."

"Such as the manly art of providing and so on?"

"Exactly. Don't forget the grilling. Grilling is very manly."

"Hmm," I say. "He did have a pretty traditional outlook in a lot of ways. Insert wife here and she does these set things. I wouldn't say he established parameters exactly, but there were expectations that could be a little constraining at times. Like he'd be surprised by some of the stuff I did. It's amazing how people can make you feel like shit without saying a word."

"It is. And I think their parents are to blame in part for painting a picture of the female of the species as either being a Madonna or whore with little in between."

"I hear you," I say. "Like mother and family and home are

all we're capable of. Or all that's fitting. I hate that shit. The idea that our role in life is solely determined by our designated sex organs instead of our brains and our hearts."

"Lots of idiot men out there feel that way."

"They need to take a look at the calendar and see what century they're living in."

"True," she says.

"I think their parents have something to answer for in helping to establish that point of view."

"Along with the person themselves needing to answer some hard questions," says Briar. "You can only blame your parents for ruining your life for so long."

"I actually quite enjoy hanging my issues on Mom sometimes."

"Hell, we've all done that. Don't feel special."

"Whatever gets you through the night," I agree. "It's nice to know that our Introduction to Psychology class can come in handy all these years later."

"Professor Callihan was something else."

"Oh, he was so hot."

"The thirst was real."

"I enjoyed that class for many and varied reasons."

"I totally respected the man for his mind," jokes Briar. "Maybe we should have taken some philosophy as well to aid us in our spouting deep and intelligent-sounding bullshit regarding each other's love lives."

I click my tongue. "Yeah. That would be something. Imagine the size of the words we could use then."

"We should start a podcast. Just us dissecting people's love lives and general life choices."

"Like everyone could benefit from our wisdom?" I ask.

"Exactly."

"God help everyone," I laugh, and she laughs, and it's all so good. Just chatting with a friend. Feeling that connection with the sisterhood and all. Clem and Tessa had asked me to accompany them to a movie sometime, but I don't know. Something held me back. As much as I liked them, I didn't want to rush into anything.

"Though getting back to the subject of woman as breeder and child wrangler." She pauses to clear her throat. "You do want to have children and there's nothing wrong with that."

"There is nothing wrong with that. It's just not all I want, you know?"

"So what do you want?" she asks, head cocked.

At this, I'm laughing again. "Oh, boy. After all of my brave words, I don't actually know. I'm still figuring it out."

"It's not over until it's over. You have time. There's no rush."

"Thanks." I wrinkle my nose, thinking deep thoughts. "Do you think I'm rushing into this, though?"

"This as in Leif?"

"Yeah. Seeing someone so soon after the divorce has given me pause. I'm sure certain people would be horrified."

"Fuck them. No, I don't think you're moving too fast," she says. "It's been months since you and that cheating fool were together as an actual couple. Don't beat yourself up over the imagined opinions of people who don't matter."

I sigh. "You're right."

"Furthermore, I think the universe sends us opportunities on its own timeline and we can either take the chance and make it work or not," she says. "There's never a perfect time to meet someone. There's always something going on or some issue in your head you should be dealing with on your own. But life keeps right on happening."

"God, you're wise."

"About some things, maybe." She narrows her eyes. "Here's a question for you . . . do you still believe in love?"

"That sounds like the start of a Cher song."

She snorts. "Don't go there."

In an act of pure avoidance, I turn the question back on her. "Tell me, Briar, do you believe in love?"

"Well, the bartender I may have mentioned a time or two certainly has given a lot of time and attention to give me. A lot of physical affection. We definitely have chemistry. It could certainly develop into something." Her tongue plays behind her cheek. "I don't know if I've ever been in love exactly. Not the kind of true, enduring, and abiding love we all hear about and they keep putting into songs and books and movies. The fact is, I was focusing on my studies and now my main priority is my job. But that doesn't mean someone couldn't come along and encourage me to make room for more. You never know."

"It's up to fate, then."

"I think it is."

"Romantic love is nice and all, but it's not like we don't have lots of other types of love in our life."

"This is also true," she says.

"Friendship, family, et cetera."

"They can all be hugely important and rewarding."

"Speaking of which, I was thinking a trip to New York around Christmastime would be nice. We could freeze our ass off in the big city."

"Really?" Her eyes light up. "I highly recommend you write that into your calendar. I would love to have you come visit. Not sure I'll be making it home again this year."

"It's decided then. We can shop and drink and so on."

"We sure can. I'll be looking forward to it." She grins. "You never did answer my question, though."

"What question?"

"Do you still believe in love?"

"I don't know," I admit. "I think relationships are hard and it's easy to coast along on the basis of not causing waves. In which case, you ultimately just sort of drift apart."

Her brows rise. "Nice boating analogies."

"I'm probably not the best person to talk to about love just yet."

"But what about the initial rush of falling in love," she asks. "Do you still believe in that?"

I stick out my tongue. "I don't know."

"Do me a favor and ask Leif what he thinks."

"What?" I semi screech.

"Just do it." And the woman hangs up on me.

I set my cell down on the dining room table and take a breath. "Hell no. That's never going to happen."

CHAPTER EIGHT

"I DON'T THINK THIS IS TRADITIONALLY HOW IT'S MEANT to be done."

"Anna, baby," he says, gesturing with his hand while doing an impressive thrust of the hips. Very Elvis. "Give me more. I don't dance for free."

Since I left my shoes at the door and I've already thrown my white embroidered button-down at him, I stand and shimmy out of my dark blue jeans. Those I kind of kick across the floor in his general direction since it would be dangerous to throw them if the belt buckle caught him in the face. I like his face how it is just fine.

"Thank you," he says and does a twirl. He's quite the dancer. That he can leer at me in my underwear while dancing at the same time is a hell of a skill.

"I like this song."

"Hozier is great."

At this point he attempts the moon walk, but I'm sad to say it doesn't quite work. Maybe he needs to try it again in just socks instead of wearing his boots. Too much grip.

"That was great," I lie encouragingly, sitting cross-legged

on the sofa in my underwear. Because why not be comfortable? Only Leif can see me and he apparently appreciates the view. This is my home now. Though this does mean the Maintaining a Reasonable Standard of Clothing in Joint Areas of the Household rule is well and truly out the window.

"I need to practice more often." He grins. Then he stops grinning and gives me his serious expression. "What'd you want to talk about?"

"Oh, right . . ."

Now he's doing the twist. And waiting for my next words. This is expressed through some come-hither-type hand movements. Unless he's doing a mangled version of the mashed potato. In all honesty, it could be either.

"Are we exclusive?" I ask, sitting up straight. Like I'm being interviewed for a job position or something. Which is silly. Maybe I shouldn't have just blurted it out, but we're never going to get anywhere if I'm not open and honest. I know that much for sure.

"Yes." And that's it. That's all he says.

"Um. Okay. You don't want to discuss it or anything?"

"Nah." He pauses. "Wait. Did you not want to be exclusive?"

"No, I do. That's fine with me."

"Good," he says. "Anything else you wanted to talk about?"

I think it over. "No."

"There's nothing else on your mind? Are you sure?"

"You mean like what are we going to have for dinner or something?"

"No," he says, with a pained expression. "I mean like the you-feeling-uncomfortable-with-me-seeing-other-women's-body-parts-sometimes-when-I work issue."

I frown. "Ed tell you about that?"

"Yeah, but he didn't need to. I could tell you weren't exactly comfortable while I was with Courtney."

Guess it's not exactly a surprise Ed told him, what with them being family and everything. But I need to bear in mind that conversations I have with him in future might be shared with Leif. Think I need to practice my poker face in general.

"You're right, I wasn't," I say. "But that's not an *us* problem."

"There's an *us*?"

I shrug.

"I'm fine with it, just curious. So. How is this not an *us* problem?"

"Whatever our relationship is, seeing body parts is part of your job," I explain. "You're not asking these women to take their clothes off in front of you for kicks."

"Of course not. I have you for that." He holds out his hand. "Bra, please."

I dutifully start wrestling with the closure. I have a serious problem saying no to this man. "Leif, I still think it's you who should be stripping for me here."

"Nah. My way is better."

"Whatever," I say, tossing the item of underwear at his head. "Get dancing then. Show me those moves."

"I really wish I'd learned 'Single Ladies' by Beyoncé. Now that would be impressive."

"It would be cool," I agree.

He starts doing a side-shuffle-type thing. The man has snake hips. They're mesmerizing really. "You were explaining why your discomfort over certain aspects of my work isn't a conversation that involves both of us despite us doing vaguely heavy-duty-relationship-type stuff these days."

"Heavy duty?"

He just shrugs.

"Well, for the simple fact that it is your work and I knew that before getting involved with you," I explain.

"And?"

"I need to get over it."

"And you can do that?" he asks. "Just get over it?"

"Yeah."

He raises a brow.

"Don't give me that look. It might take me a little while, but I will indeed get over it." I laze back on the couch, getting comfortable. Oh the sweet relief of taking your bra off after a long day. So good. And apart from the occasional dip of his gaze to my chest, he's doing an excellent job of keeping his focus on my face while we talk. "The fact is, we're roommates with benefits. We're exclusive sex friends, fuck buddies, stuff like that. I don't have the right to demand you make any major life changes for me. Even if I felt I did have the right, asking you to no longer perform certain aspects of your work because I was uncomfortable would be unreasonable."

"Huh. Okay. Panties, please." He holds a hand out, clicking his fingers.

"This is ridiculous. You're fully dressed."

He shakes his head all sad like. "Hey, I don't make the rules. I just ask that you politely and promptly follow them."

"You do so make the rules."

"Give me the panties, Anna. Don't make me ask again."

"This is my point exactly," I grumble. Then I raise my hips

and shimmy the panties off too. Nice, sensible white cotton underwear again. If the man wants fancy then he can provide some. These days, comfort is my thing.

"I think you like me taking control sometimes," he says with a certain look in his eyes.

"Is that so?"

"Yep."

I think it over. "Maybe. Sometimes."

"It's nothing to be ashamed of."

"I'm not ashamed. Just never thought of it that way."

"It's kind of a trust issue, right?" he asks, twirling my panties on a finger. Like a pervert. "I mean, either you trust me not to do anything you wouldn't be okay with or not. Both in bed when we're messing around and at work when I'm tattooing."

I shrug. Trust isn't really a topic I'm keen on discussing for various reasons. "As for work, you're in the back room generally for these types of jobs. I can't keep an eye on you. Nor do I want to. I'm not your mother. I'm not even your girlfriend."

"Eh," he says.

I'm leaving that one alone. We've only been sleeping together for a short while, for heaven's sake. There's no rush. Not with everything that we've both been through. Maybe he'll decide he doesn't really want to be with me. That it's too complicated or something. So we'll retire to our separate bedrooms and go back to being just friends. It could happen. Lacking a crystal ball and any psychic powers, I have no idea of what the future holds. Except the thought of us taking a step back from the intimacy we have now hurts my heart. And my loins. Let's be honest here. When a man has the power to talk you out of your clothes on the thinnest of pretexts, something is definitely going on. Sitting bare-ass on the sofa, I can admit this much.

"Anyway, this is all very mature and understanding of you, Anna."

"Thank you."

"I've had varied reactions from women I've dated. But none that were actually right there and had to see it happening," he says. "Sort of. I mean, you were in the next room and all."

"I get it."

"Have to remember that you might be a bit younger than me, but you're way ahead of me in relationship experience."

"Long-term relationship experience, maybe."

"Yeah, that."

I cross my legs and receive the heaviest of frowns.

"No," he says. "Spread 'em."

"I'm not spreading my legs."

He continues to sway his hips in time to the music. "Please?"

"No."

"Pretty please?"

"Still no." I laze back against the couch, bracing my head with one hand. "Reciprocity, buddy. Show me some skin."

"That's not the way this game goes," he says, voice fake outraged.

"You want me to go get my robe?"

He rolls his eyes and tucks my panties in his back pocket. No idea if I'll be getting those back later. Then he finally at long last thank God tugs off his T-shirt. Oh yeah, baby. This is what I'm talking about. The right to now ogle him guilt free is a beautiful thing. I can stare and stare to my heart's delight. Maybe I'll even snap a picture or two with his permission. The strong lines of his arms and upper chest are enchanting. The dips and planes of his six-pack. For certain, all of the running with his brother and midnight exercise sessions have paid off and then some. The man is a visual delight. Without being asked, he toes off his boots and tugs off his socks. This necessitates a pause in the dancing lest he fall on his gorgeous ass. Which would be sad.

I never got to play before. Not like this. I like playing with Leif very much.

And the growing hard-on tenting the front of his jeans is a joy to see. In all honesty, he makes my mouth water and my thighs clench. There'd definitely be a party in my pants if I were in fact wearing any. Because my want to tackle him and take him to the ground is intense. To have my wicked way with the man. To suck on his neck and mark him as mine like some feral teenager in the backseat of a car. Then all of the Courtneys in the world would know exactly who he belongs to. Good God. He's making me primal. A wild thing.

"Do you trust me?" He pauses and cocks his head. "That's got to be a big thing for you, right?"

I blink. Changing my thought process from dick-struck to decision-making takes a moment. A long, hard one. Ha-ha.

"After everything that soggy ball-sack did to you, you've got to have some real issues around trust," he says.

Ugh. And there's that word again. "Do we have to talk about this right now?"

"I think we should." The damn tease toys with the top button on his jeans. "Don't you? It's only fair. You got to ask an *us* question and now it's my turn."

"Fine. Whatever."

"Spread your legs, by the way."

"No," I say. "If we're talking about my issues then my legs are staying closed for now. Allow me some defensive maneuvers."

He thinks it over for a moment. "I strongly disagree with that decision, but okay. Talk to me, Anna."

"Oh, man," I groan, my head falling back against the couch. "I trust you with certain things, okay? It's complicated."

"Huh."

"What?"

"I don't think I've ever had a woman lay that one on me before. 'It's complicated,'" he says. "I know I've used it a couple of times, but never actually gotten it thrown back at me."

"It's the truth."

He nods. "I know. I get it."

"Can we stop talking about this now?" I ask. "Please?"

"Not quite yet. Just out of interest, what things do you trust me with?"

I sigh. "I don't know. I trust you as a friend."

"But not as a lover?"

"I trust you not to hurt or humiliate me in bed. To make sure I have a good time."

"That's good," he says. "I'm glad you're at ease with me when we're having sex. But I take it trust out of bed is going to take longer?"

I don't know what to say.

"Your heart's locked up tight, huh?" It's more of a statement than a question. And important to note, he's not saying he wants my heart. More like he's testing my limits or something. This new dalliance of ours is so confusing.

"Leif," I say, voice low and a little anguished. "We just started this."

"Right, right." He gives me his best fake smile. Guess it's been a day for those. "I understand."

"I'm sorry. I don't want to hurt you."

"I get that." He takes a breath. "You know I'll always do my best to be careful with you, don't you? Tell me that much is clear."

"Yes."

His smile turns into something more real. Something with actual warmth. "You wouldn't believe how many times today I thought about your pussy."

"Is that so?"

"Yeah," he says. "I've seen some pretty vaginas in my lifetime, but yours is beautiful."

"Ah, thank you."

He scratches at his stubble all contemplative like. "It's actually on the verge of becoming an occupational hazard, my obsession with your pussy. If I'm not careful I might lose track of what I'm doing and someone might accidentally wind up with your clitoris tattooed on their shoulder. Your labia inked out on their leg. Who knows?"

I laugh. "Oh my, God."

"I did a quick sketch during my lunch break if you'd like to see it."

"Of my . . ."

"Of your cunt. Yes."

"You did not." Heat rushes into my face. "Leif."

He just grins.

"You're joking." I sag in relief.

"Am I?" he asks, acting all coy. Bastard.

"This is the strangest discussion I've ever had."

"I thought about you all day long," he says.

"A part of me."

"All of you really. I was just messing with you." He tips his chin. "Come over here."

"So you didn't really draw my . . ."

"Oh yeah, I did. I was serious about that," he says. "But I haven't just been fixating on just one part. It's more the whole of you that's making me happy."

"Is that so?" And there's this warmth inside of me. Like my heart is too big for my chest. I don't want to feel so much, but I can't help it. He does things to me. "I thought about you too."

"Good to hear."

I cross the floor, fingers itching to touch the man. I'm such a fool for him and I couldn't stop it now if I tried. That's the truth. All of my anxiety and second-guessing is for nothing. I'm holding onto this thing between us for as long as I can. My hands slide down his chest, taking in all of his hot, smooth skin.

"I like it when you're bold," he says in a deep voice. "When you take what you want."

"So do I."

"There's no judgment here, baby. You can do whatever you like. Have whatever you want." He licks his lips and heat rushes through me.

"Leif . . ."

"Hmm?"

"Enough already with the pants." My smile is all sharp teeth as I tear into the button and fly of his jeans. With the material bunched up, I push them halfway down his thighs. Past his spectacular tight ass and all the rest.

"What can I do you for, Anna?"

"Just stay still."

A brief frown of confusion crosses his face.

"It's my turn to give," I say, sinking to my knees.

While there's a definite art to sucking cock, any man worth your time is just going to be happy you want to use your mouth on him. That's the fact of the matter. Still, I lick my lips and gaze up at him.

This whole situation gives me a thrill. From the hard wooden floor beneath my knees to the cool night air on my bare skin. For all he says I like giving up control, it's hard not to feel like I have all of the power with my teeth so close to his dick. A wicked thought, but I don't back away from it. All of this is a revelation. This is what it's like to enjoy someone fully, to be safe with them. I never realized how it was missing, how much I wanted it, until Leif started giving it to me. Though I don't say it, I hope he feels cherished. Wanted. Adored. I want that for him with all my heart and soul because he's been through more than enough. We both have.

"Okay?" I ask.

His nod is terse, his hands fisted in anticipation.

I grab hold of his half-hard cock and give it a few pumps. The solid heat and velvet of him is intoxicating. Especially combined with his musky, salty scent. And I know he's going to taste the same. The dark of his pupils are so large I think I could drown in them. As if I could lose myself in the way he's watching me. Like I'm everything he could ever want. Same as always, it's a dizzying sensation, receiving all of this man's focus. Having the whole world narrowed down to this moment, to just him and me. It's like he's magic, the way he does this to me each and every time.

My mouth waters and my heart pounds as I guide him to

my lips. I drag the flat of my tongue over the head of his cock again and again, getting him wet. Then I take just a little into my mouth, tracing the rim of his cockhead with the tip of my tongue. He sucks in a breath, letting it out slow. I swear the man doesn't even blink. When I suck on him good and hard, his jaw goes rigid. My hands work the rest of him, one fondling his balls and massaging his perineum while the other tightens and tugs on the thick length of him. I lick him and drag my lips down as much of his length as I can manage. Loving him with my mouth. Giving him my all. And it's nothing less than delightful to see his thigh muscles bulge as he fights to stay still, to stay upright.

"Fuck," he says, gruff and deep.

After a few more minutes of this, he can't hold out any longer. His stomach muscles tightening and eyelids squeezing shut. Veins stand out beneath the velvet skin and his balls draw up tight to his body. Beads of pre-cum hit my tongue.

"I'm close," he hisses, giving me warning.

And when he does go, losing all control and fucking my face with vigor, I swallow over and over. Doing my best to take it all in. To take all of him. An expression somewhere between rapture and torment takes him over. It's nice to be appreciated. When at last he's finished, I ease up, being sweet, pressing a kiss to the head of his cock before letting go. His whole body is sort of slumped. And the look in his eyes . . .

"You liked it," I say, with a smile.

"*Like* is far too tame a word." Hands beneath my armpits, he hauls me to my feet and plants a kiss on my lips. His hands cup my face, gentle but firm. "Thank you."

"Thank you for being here with me."

"Oh, baby," he says, gaze full of something I'm not ready to label. "Anytime, Anna."

If I wasn't awake before the hand smacked me in the shoulder, I certainly am after. Head foggy with sleep, I switch on the bedside lamp. Leif is thrashing about on the bed. He's making these heartbreaking wounded sounds. Not words, exactly. Something else. And it's horrible. But the startled, partly muffled yell is even worse.

"Hey, Leif," I say, shaking his arm. Carefully keeping my distance just in case. "Leif. Babe, it's okay. Come on, wake up. You're having a dream. It's just a dream."

His eyelids blink open, his gaze dark and confused as he looks around.

"Are you all right?" I ask.

"Anna?"

"Yeah." I switch from shaking his arm to petting it. Long, gentle caresses of his feverish hot skin. I smooth his hair back from his face, touching him slow and sweet. Doing my best to soothe him. This is the first bad dream I've been present for and it was a doozy. "Must have been a hell of a nightmare."

A grunt from him.

"Was it about the accident?"

He winces, then nods.

"Do you want to talk about it?"

"No."

"Can I get you a glass of water or anything? Is there anything I can do to help?"

For a moment, he just stares at me. Only the streetlight

creeping around the curtain's edges provides any light. The night is silent now that he's woken. Perfectly still. Apart from the harsh breaths pumping in and out of his chest. Whatever he saw has freaked him right out.

"C'mere," he says, opening his arms. I stretch out at his side, resting my head on his shoulder. Eventually, he says, "First one I've had since we started sleeping together."

"Yeah." And it feels like a failure, that I couldn't fix this for him, but that's stupid. It doesn't help anybody. Lacking superpowers or mystical abilities, all I can do is be there for the man. And that I intend to do with my whole heart.

His arms wrap me up tight, his jawline resting against the top of my head. Slowly, steadily, his breathing calms. Against my hip, his fingers tense and release, over and over again. "You were stuck in the car and . . . I couldn't get the motorbike off me. My arm was all fucked up and the bike was so damn heavy I just couldn't shift it. I was trapped."

Reaching up, I stroke his jawline. The harsh stubble leading to the softer skin.

"I couldn't get to you."

I inch up until our faces are on the same level. Until we're looking at each other. And there's a haunted expression in his eyes that I hate. Nice and gentle, I press my lips to his in a show of benediction. A blessing mixed with gratitude. But one of his hands grabs the back of my head, holding me to him for something longer, deeper. And I'm happy to give.

"You've got me," I say.

"Have I?"

"I'm right here and I'm not going anywhere."

Nothing from him.

"The accident was horrible and it hurt us, but we survived. We got out of there."

He lets out a deep breath. "Okay."

I rest my head back on his shoulder, holding on tight. I didn't even have the nightmare and I'm scared and shaken. Maybe it's seeing Leif so affected. I don't know.

"I think you should talk to someone about these dreams," I say.

Immediately he tenses beneath me. "Anna, no."

"Fine. Whatever. Maybe we should go to couple's therapy, though. I have some concerns."

"I thought you said we weren't a couple."

"No," I say. "I said our relationship was complicated."

"Ah."

"But on the off chance we become a serious couple we'd already have the therapy out of the way. Imagine how healthy our relationship would be!"

He makes a noise in his throat. Disbelief, perhaps. "Is this the sort of couple's therapy where you drag me along on the pretext of it being about us communicating and then make me talk about my nightmares to a professional?"

"Maybe," I admit. "All right, yes. But would that really be so bad?"

Nothing from him.

"And it would be amongst discussing our other issues, of course."

"Such as?"

"Well . . ."

"I'm waiting," he says, voice on the verge of cranky. This is clearly a difficult topic for him.

"There's my penchant for being judgy to be considered," I say. "I can be quite the highfalutin bitch when I set my mind to it, as you've noticed on several occasions."

He snorts. "You're not so bad."

"And then there's my trust issues. We could work on those."

With a heavy sigh, he draws a line with his fingers up and down my spine. "Anna . . ."

"It's just a thought."

"I know."

I search my mind for the right thing to say and come up empty. Probably because it's like two in the morning.

"I thought we weren't rushing things between us," he says. "Couple's therapy not even a week into our roommates-with-benefits relationship seems like a hell of a leap."

"But it could take months to actually get in to see a good therapist."

A grunt from him.

I just let the silence linger. Right up until I can't. My mind is going a mile a minute. "The psychologist in the hospital that I talked to really helped me get things sorted out. To manage my expectations and adjust to the new way of things. To overcome the trauma of it all."

"That's good. I'm glad."

"Yeah."

"But the dreams will go away eventually," he says. Not even sounding convinced himself. If anything, he seems tired, hurt, and defeated. "I don't need anyone messing around with the inside of my head."

"It's coming up on a year since the accident," I say in a gentle voice.

"That's still a ways off."

"It's not that far."

"Hmm," he says. "I don't know."

"Just think about it. I'll make it worth your while."

"Oh, yeah?"

"Totally," I say, shuffling up and around until I can nuzzle the side of his face. "I am more than open to bribing you, baby."

"I'm all ears."

"Like, I'll share my skincare routine with you."

"Wow," he says in a flat voice.

"Right?" I smile. "That shit's taken me years to get down and here I am just offering it up for free."

"I cleanse and moisturize."

"Yeah, but do you chemically exfoliate before applying a serum, eye cream, hydrating gel, and moisturizer mixed with facial oil for enhanced hydration?"

"Can't say that I do."

"There you go. Amateur." It's official. Nibbling on Leif's neck is now my new favorite thing. "I wonder if a therapist would think our attachment was unhealthy due to us meeting through the accident and everything."

"Where the hell did that come from?" he asks, back to sounding cranky again. Whoops.

"I don't know. Just a random thought."

"That's it. We're not going to therapy," he says. "We each have enough hang-ups without that sort of negativity entering into things."

"They might not say we're unhealthy. You never know. I was just overthinking things."

"Mm." He says nothing for a moment. "Do you worry about that? About our friendship being unhealthy?"

"I didn't really until now."

Which is when he rolls me beneath his big body with minimal effort. "New household rule, Anna. No coming up with new problems until we've dealt with the ones we have already, okay?"

"That makes sense, I guess."

"I know you're a worrier, but we have to keep things in check or we're both going to get overwhelmed."

"Okay." I lick my suddenly dry lips. "Maybe I should just not say everything that goes through my head."

"I like you sharing. Just . . . take it easy. All right?"

I nod.

"Good. Thank you. And now for the sex."

"Again?" I whine and pout just because. Makes it hard not to giggle when his mouth latches onto one nipple and his hands starts creeping between our bodies, making for my vagina.

"You're the one who wanted to get her experience levels up," he says. "Don't blame me. This is all your own damn fault. Like there aren't other things I could be doing with my time right now."

"Fine. But I'm very tired. Don't blame me if I fall asleep."

Which is about when he bites my breast. The man has teeth. Fortunately for him he also has a tongue to soothe the sting. Neither of us have any nightmares again that night. Though, to be fair, we don't actually get much sleep.

CHAPTER NINE

"**W**HAT IS THAT LOOK FOR?" I ask, stirring a spoonful of sugar into my coffee.

Mom continues giving me a sly smile. As if she's super pleased with herself or something.

"Mother, explain yourself."

She crosses her legs, getting comfy at the quiet corner table we scored at a busy café. We've already visited Clem and her boss, Iris, at Braun's Books. Both Mom and I now own a healthy selection of romance novels. Considering it was Clem who gave *Twilight* to Leif to read to me while I was in a coma, the least we can do is support her awesome local indie bookstore. It's been a nice day with beautiful warm weather. Perfect for wandering around town. I can't remember the last time we did something like this. She and I spending time out and about that's not related to the accident or some family gathering. Just being together. At least I don't have to worry about her stabbing me in the back or anything like that. Mom is a much safer option than most.

"Oh, it's nothing," she says. "I just happened to be talking to Leif the other day is all."

"I find it so disturbing that you two are friends," I say.

She frowns. "Why?"

"Because he's half your age, male, and a tattoo artist. For starters."

"Nonsense," she says with a wave of her hand. "Our differences just mean we have more to discuss and offer each other in the way of new experiences and altered perspectives."

"Right. What does Dad say about your friendship?"

She gives me an amused glance. "What possible business is it of his who I'm friends with?"

"Actually, you have a very valid point there."

"Our marriage is fine. He would hardly imagine I'm about to run off and have a wild fling now, would he?"

"I guess not," I say. Though she does seem to be enjoying the attention of an older male not so covertly watching us from across the room. Everyone likes to feel attractive or special now and then, I guess.

"Admit it, you just don't want to share your friend with me."

"That makes me sound like a six-year-old fighting over a Barbie doll," I say, somewhat put out.

Mom just looks at me.

"Fine. Be friends with him. I don't care."

"Thank you for your permission, dear," she says, lips pursed. "There's a special sort of bond that comes with someone willing to sit for hours at my unconscious daughter's bedside and read to her. I have a lot of respect for that boy."

"Man."

"You know what I mean."

"I do," I say. "Carry on."

"He was in a great deal of pain what with his arm, and he still managed to display more of a caring nature toward you than your husband managed in months of getting in the nurses' way and generally feeling sorry for himself." She pauses to frown at the memory. "At any rate, I was delighted to hear that you and Leif are doing so well."

It's been two weeks since he and I became intimate. Bed friends. Roommates with benefits. Sexual partners. Whatever. We work together, sleep together, and eat most meals together. We're also having an insane amount of fun in and out of the bedroom. Proving that we can actually spend time apart, he's having lunch with his family while I have a Sunday afternoon visit with my mother. While he did invite me to lunch at his parents', I demurred. It's too soon. Too big a step. What if they didn't like me? Ryan's mother only tolerated me at best. Though I'm not sure anyone would have been good enough for her golden boy. What if Leif's parents met me and hated me and told him he'd be better off without me? I wasn't ready to set myself up for failure in that way. To add that sort of strain to things. Besides which, Mom wanted to see the condo and where I work. It's been nice to catch up with her. Until now.

"Wait," I say. "What's that meant to mean? 'Doing so well'?"

"Well, that you're together."

"He told you that? That we're together?"

"Hmm?" Mom delicately takes a bite of her cookie before pressing the paper napkin to her lips. "Of course not. Rest assured, he doesn't give away any of your secrets. He's not stupid."

"Then why would you think . . ."

"Know, dear. I *know* that you two are now together," she says. "And that's because I could hear it in his tone of voice when he talks about you. The boy was practically gushing. It was so sweet."

"The boy is over thirty years old."

Mom just shrugs. "I do find it interesting that you're not denying that you and he are now involved."

"What would be the point?" I take a sip of coffee. "You're already convinced you're right."

"That's because I am right."

"I've neither confirmed nor denied."

"You don't need to. I already know."

I smile despite myself. "Yeah, well, it's not serious, so don't get carried away and start planning another wedding."

"Look at that smile. You're happy and it's beautiful to see. As for planning anything, I wouldn't dare," she says in a sassy tone. "And I'd imagine you're taking your time and getting to know one another, which is wise and good. There's no need to rush into anything."

I just nod.

"Just enjoy yourself. You haven't been single for a long time. There's all these opportunities and possibilities available to you right now."

"The ink on the divorce certificate is still fresh. Whatever would the church ladies say?"

She clicks her tongue. "Everyone has an opinion, Anna. Doesn't mean you need to listen."

"True."

"Good Lord, you admitting I'm right about something. Pinch me. Am I really awake?"

I give her the look. "At least I come by my sarcastic tendencies honestly."

Mom laughs.

"How's Dad?"

"Alive and well. He's off playing golf."

"Of course he is," I mumble. "Does that ever bother you, how much time and effort goes into golf?"

Mom sits back in her chair with her legs crossed, rocking her foot back and forth. "No, not for my part. We both have our own interests, which is good. Otherwise we'd have nothing to talk about. We heard all of each other's stories a long time ago. Not that I have any particular interest in hearing about his golf game, but I'm glad it makes him happy and opens him up to a new social group."

"Okay."

"Your father and I have always done our best communicating in bed."

My brows shoot up. "Oh, God. You did not just tell me that."

"One thing I've learned is that you have to choose what kind of relationship you want," she continues. "If you send them off with a smile then there's a better chance that they'll rush on back to you when they're done with whatever. Oh, and the second thing I learned was to pick your fights. If you want your voice to be heard, then use it wisely."

"I basically agree with those. But what about venting in general? Are you just supposed to shut up and play the good wife and never say a thing?"

"No. That's different."

"Ah."

"It's interesting, isn't it, looking at how people relate," says Mom. "I always say, you have no idea what makes or doesn't make a relationship work unless you're one of the people in it."

"That makes sense."

Back and forth rocks her foot. "Don't lose your nerve just because of one failed marriage. Your Aunt Peggy didn't find Mister Right until her third try."

"And you mocked her for it."

"Did I?" Mom frowns off into the middle distance. "I don't remember that."

"It was mostly done behind her back."

"Hmm," she says. "The years may have softened me some. So has almost losing my only child. If anything is going to teach you grace and how not to sweat the small stuff, it's that. But I'll have you know that I also took Peggy in and let her sleep in our spare room for months at a time when marriages one and two fell apart. I'm not totally terrible."

"I never said you were."

"You wouldn't believe how many long-winded discussions we had over a bottle of wine late at night after you'd gone to bed."

"Family is complicated."

"Well, that's true. I don't think there's anything wrong with being a little teasing now and then. Or with venting."

"This conversation has gotten unexpectedly deep and probing."

"Is that a problem?" she asks.

"No. Just a bit surprising. Why did we never talk this openly before?"

She contemplates this for a moment, stirring the spoon around in her coffee once again. "Maybe Ryan and Celine didn't leave much room in your life for other people."

"Hmm."

"Or maybe I was busy with my own things and didn't make enough of an effort with you."

"Maybe we both needed to make more of an effort," I say.

"Maybe. Perhaps you were also a little wary of me. I heaped a lot of expectations on you when you were younger. I was harder on you than I should have been because you were a girl. A lot of it was about me and the way I grew up. What type of a parent my own mother was to me. It was only when I saw how it was hurting you that I realized and stopped. But time teaches us all to calm the heck down some. To be kinder to yourself and others," she says with a gentle smile. "I'm sorry I wasn't always the best mother, sweetie. I learned from my mistakes, but that doesn't change the fact that mistakes were made. I'm sorry they hurt you, and I want you to know I love you more than anything."

"I love you too, Mom, and neither of us are perfect. Thanks for all you've done to help me get back on my feet."

"When I thought I lost you in the accident, I'd never been more terrified."

"It was no one's idea of a good time, that's for sure."

"Still, no one could blame you for being a little defensive right now. A little on edge. But try not to let it become a habit. None of us are perfect. Don't be so hard on yourself."

I sigh, wishing that it were that simple. Today's been

wonderful, but I still feel like I'm always just one breath, one moment, away from collapsing into that brittle, messy piece of work left over from the accident. I don't know why some times it hits harder than others. Guess healing comes in bits and pieces. It stops and starts and takes you by surprise. Leif would understand all this. But then, Leif always understands. And right in this moment, I'd give anything to have him here to hold my hand. And that sort of weakness scares me.

I swallow hard. "You're very wise, Mother."

"Sometimes." She takes a sip of coffee. "At least we're open to being wrong and doing better. That's a good thing. Most people never even get that far."

"I love you, you know?"

"I know, sweetie. I love you too. Drink your coffee before it goes cold."

It's getting on toward sunset by the time I arrive home. Coffee turned into a glass of wine, which turned into dinner. Mom and I had a great time. Maybe it takes a while before you see your parents as being real people. Someone other than your designated caregiver and eternal judge. Someone capable of making mistakes and having regrets. Instead of just being the person who has to listen to you moan and groan and drive you places and who will hopefully take you in if everything in your life hits the wall. What it says about me that it took me so long to see her as a real live functioning entity separate from being my maternal figure probably isn't good. But at least I got there in the end. Mom and I are more than just mother and daughter now. We're friends too, and that's beautiful.

I also managed to calm my roll and find my inner peace once more. Everything is okay. Everything is going to be fine. Probably. And that's about as certain as life gets, in all honesty. Things happen. Sometimes they're unexpected and painful and horrible. But I can't go through life just waiting to get knocked down again. That's not living. I will be brave and not cower in constant fear of the pain and turmoil life can throw at me. I swear it.

"Anna?"

I turn to find Ryan stepping out of his car. His expression, at first hesitant, soon turns into the usual set-jaw study of entitlement. We stand underneath the dogwood outside the condo building, staring at one another. And I am not smiling.

"What are you doing here?" I ask.

"I thought we could talk."

The man looks rumpled. His polo shirt is creased and his chino shorts are no better. Quite the change from his usual immaculate presentation of all-around great guy. It's kind of weird that I used to find him attractive. I mean, he is fundamentally an attractive person. People used to tell me how lucky I was, back when we were married. Gosh, your husband is so handsome and all that. Guess I just can't see it anymore. Overlaid on the classic chiseled-jaw features are so many memories. Mostly recent and bad. None that I feel the need to deal with right here and now. Or ever.

"No, we're divorced," I say. "There's nothing left to say."

He shoves a hand through his hair. "Anna . . ."

"Divorced means I am no longer legally required to listen to you."

And he actually looks to heaven at this. What a dick. What did I ever see in this guy?

"I'm not being unreasonable or irrational, Ryan. So don't give me that look. Your dedication to being the actual worst is amazing."

"Real mature, Anna. If you'd just—"

"No. No way."

"You've changed," he says, all thoughtful like for a moment. And whatever this change in me is, it does not please him.

"I'd certainly hope so." I take a deep breath. "What the hell did you think you were going to accomplish by coming here? Seriously?"

Then he just spits it out: "Celine was a mistake."

"Holy shit." My eyes feel as wide as twin moons. "Did you just call the mother of your unborn child a mistake?"

His lips disappear into a thin pissed-off line. "You know I don't mean it like that. But the pregnancy has made her crazy. She's making all of these outrageous demands. This is . . . we don't belong together, she and I. You and I, we used to be good together. She's not like you."

"That's true. I believe in pesky things like loyalty and stuff."

Across the street, a dude is sitting in his car watching us and fair enough. We're quite the spectacle.

"Please, be serious." He reaches out to grab hold of my arm. "Anna, we need to talk."

"Anything you need to say to me can be said through the lawyers."

"Anna!"

"And barking my name at me won't get you shit, Ryan. Now move your hand."

"Just listen for a minute, would you?"

"Get your fucking hand off of her," growls Leif, appearing behind me. Dressed in his jogging gear, so it makes sense that Ed's now here too and also witnessing this debacle.

"I've got this," I say, only no one's listening.

"This is nothing to do with you," snarls Ryan.

Leif steps closer. "Now I really have to fucking disagree with you there, buddy."

"Leif, please," I say through gritted teeth. "I can handle this."

Standing tall, my moron ex's nostrils flare and he says, "She's my wife."

"What?" asks Leif, tone outraged.

"Not even close, Ryan." And now I'm using my pointing finger. Never a good sign. "What the hell is wrong with you? Are you delusional? Did you actually just say that I'm your *wife*? And you had the gall to use the present tense?"

He doesn't respond.

"There aren't enough words to describe how very wrong you are right now."

Ryan's furious gaze takes in Leif standing so close to my back and oh boy. The penny drops. I can see it in Ryan's eyes the minute he realizes that Leif and I are involved. That I've moved on, at least sexually. An expression of hurt crosses my ex's face for a moment, and give me a damn break. I'm not cheating. Not even remotely. But his pain morphs straight into anger, and now it's well and truly on. Testosterone all but scents the air and oh my God.

With a strangled sound, Ryan lets go of me and swings at Leif's face, clipping his jaw. Leif stumbles back a step before launching himself at my ex. In the midst of all this, I'm pushed aside by said ex, but manage to land on my ass in the nice soft grass. The two grown men, however, are busy rolling around, battling it out like we're in the damn schoolyard. Fists fly and punches land. Grunts and groans fill the air. Holy hell. This cannot be happening.

"Are you okay?" Ed kneels at my side.

"Yeah," I say, my eyes itching with unshed tears. And they're not for me and my sore ass. "Can you stop these idiots, please?"

Before answering, he assists me in getting back on my feet. "Sure thing, Anna."

And he breaks up the battling duo by waiting until Ryan is on top, then hauling him up by the back of his polo. He dispenses of my raging ex by throwing him into some nearby shrubbery. A very scratchy landing. Meanwhile, to his brother he offers a hand. Leif's eye is swollen and a dark bruise blossoms on his chin. What a mess.

"Are you hurt?" I say, rushing to his side.

"No. Are you?"

I shake my head.

Ryan pulls himself out of the shrubbery. "I'm calling the police."

"You fucking—" starts Leif.

I hold up a hand. "I've got this. Please listen when I say that this time."

Leif shuts his mouth, gaze suddenly wary. The man is not stupid.

"You're going to call the cops about a fight you started, Ryan?" I ask, dealing with the situation as promised. "Really? How do you think that's going to go?"

His face is set in mulish lines, his hair ruffled, and nose dripping blood. It looks broken. The line of it wrong somehow. Can't say he didn't deserve that.

"Leif was only defending himself. Not to mention, you also pushed me, Ryan," I say. "Me. The ex-wife you just went through a pretty damn acrimonious divorce with. You made me fall. Pretty sure that counts as assault, don't you?"

He sets his hands on his hips, giving me a distinctly pissy expression. The nerve of this bastard.

"Shall I press charges or are you going to stop being an idiot, peacefully leave, and promise never to return? Or would you like to end the day needing a criminal lawyer as well as a divorce lawyer?" I ask.

Something close to panic enters his gaze. "Anna, wait, please. I didn't mean to hurt you."

"You never do," I say. "And yet you still make the worst damn choices. I'm done being hurt by you. And I'm done letting you hurt the people I care about."

"I'm sorry." Oh the angst. He's giving it his all. "I just wanted to talk."

"Oh, Jesus. Give me strength." I take in a deep breath. "Listen to me, Ryan. Are you listening?"

"Yes."

"We are never, not in a million years, getting back together. Do you hear me? Are you taking this in?"

He opens his mouth to speak, but I get there first.

"I don't want to hear anything you have to say. You and everything to do with you is behind me now. I couldn't mean it more if I tried, Ryan," I say. "The divorce was neither a cry for help nor a plea for your attention. There are no do-overs or second chances. We're done. Finished. Kaput. Never again do I want you to darken my doorstep. Now kindly get the fuck out of here."

For a moment his face blanks, incredulous. Over the message, my choice of language, or a combination of both, I don't know. Then he about-faces and stomps off to his car. The door opens, he climbs in, then slams the door shut. The engine turns on and he drives off with the screeching of tires. Oh thank God for that.

I slump in relief.

"On a scale of one to ten, how pissed are you at me right now?" asks Leif in a somewhat concerned voice. Also, he's still covered in bruises, which I hate.

"You scared me. You could have been seriously injured."

"Nah," he drawls. "By that sad sack of shit? Never. I can take him. Another minute and I'd have . . . I'm saying the wrong thing, aren't I?"

"Yes." My mouth is flat and unimpressed. "Do not be a cool dude right now. My nerves are way too raw to handle it."

"Sorry."

"Do you want some ice for that shiner?" asks Ed.

"Nah, I'll see to it later," says Leif.

Ed looks back and forth between the two of us. "Well, if you two are okay, I might give you some space and head off."

"Yeah," says Leif. "Thanks."

Ed nods and jogs off down the road. Happy to get the hell away from the couple-fight vibes we're no doubt giving off by the bucket load.

"Do you even know why you're in trouble?" I ask.

"Um. Well . . ." He gingerly touches his swollen lip and is rewarded with a wince. "You sort of said you could handle it and ah . . ."

"Go on."

"I didn't like the way he was talking to you."

I say nothing.

"Hated the way he grabbed you," he continues. "That was really way the fuck out of line."

I cock my head. "And yet we're discussing your involvement in the incident, not his."

"You wanted me to let you handle it and I didn't," he admits finally, meeting my eyes.

"That's right."

He slowly nods. "So you're really pissed, huh?"

"No." I sigh. "More worried about you than angry. And don't give me that tough-guy crap again. Violence neither impresses me nor turns me on."

"Got it. It's been like a decade since I've been in a fistfight, honestly. Oh, no, about eight years. I forgot about that one time . . . at any rate, it's not something I tend to go around making a habit out of," he says. "That's the point I'm making here."

"I'm very glad to hear that. This situation should never

recur, but if it does, please let me decide how to handle my ex-husband in the future." I square my shoulders. "I realize him grabbing me was a long way from okay, but I had things under control."

"Understood. But if it ever goes any further than that . . . I can't stand by and let you get hurt. You understand that, right?" he asks. "I'm not trying to start anything or act like a dick, I'm just stating a fact."

"Yes, I understand. Though I don't think it would ever come to that."

"No one does until it happens. He's not exactly behaving in a rational manner these days, is he?"

I blow out a breath. "No."

"So you'll be careful, right?"

"Yes."

He goes to smile, then stops because of his poor face. "You know, Clem goes to a self-defense class every week. She shows us some of her moves sometimes, and I bet she'd have had that jerk in line in a flash. Much better than amateur hour with me. Maybe if you were ever interested you could give it a go?"

"I'll think about it."

"Please do. Because the thought of him hurting you or something else happening to you and me not being there to protect you is doing my head in."

"Leif. I'm okay. We're both fine . . . apart from some marks."

"Yeah." He hangs his head, reaching out to take hold of one of my hands. "Are you sure you're okay, Anna?"

"My butt may be slightly bruised. But otherwise I'm good."

"You don't want to check with a doctor just in case?"

"Not necessary," I say. "The ground was soft. It wasn't much of a fall. And I'll write down everything that happened just in case we need details in the future. Guess I should check with my lawyer to see what the protocol is for dealing with him harassing me."

"Very good idea. There's also security cameras covering all around the building and the front street since Clem got attacked out here. We'll ask for a copy of today's events, huh?"

"Yes. Definitely."

"Okay." He wraps his arms around me, resting his forehead lightly against mine. "We're okay."

"Your jaw and your eye are hurt."

"Eh," he says. Such a tough guy.

"What the hell must your brother think?"

"That your ex-husband is a raging asshole. But then he pretty much already knew that from the last time Ryan stopped by."

"That's true," I concede.

"Ed knows this isn't on you. Try not to worry," he says, escorting me up the steps and to the door.

It's good to get inside away from prying eyes. Even better to close the condo door behind us and lock the whole world outside. The cool calm of home is a soothing balm on my frazzled nerves.

"We need to get some ice on your face," I say.

"Hold on." He steers me toward the table. "Do me a favor and lean over."

"What?"

All of a sudden he's on his knees behind me. His hands start pushing up the skirt of my light summer dress, exposing my panties. Then my underwear is dragged halfway down my thighs exposing my ass to one and all, but mostly just to him.

"What are you doing?" I ask.

"Checking your butt." Warm fingers slide over the skin there. "It's a little-known specialty of mine. I am in fact a derriere doctor of some renown."

"Is that so?"

"Yeah. But the only ass I want to see is yours," he says, with a smile in his voice. "In fact, I'm willing to make a thorough study of these babies. These pale orbs of loveliness."

I laugh.

"I can see a red mark, but nothing serious. You're good to go." He cups his hands over my ass cheeks, giving them a pat or something. I honestly don't know what he's doing down there. But he certainly does seem committed to the cause.

"Thank you for checking," I say. On the curve of one ass cheek, he gives me a kiss. "Leif, this is very strange. What are you up to back there?"

"We've now progressed to the ass-kissing apology stage of things."

"Ah."

He wraps his hands around my hips and presses his face to the small of my back. "I'm sorry you were worried. I'll try harder to keep my temper in check when it comes to that sad sack of shit."

"Thank you."

"God knows, I'd come running back like my pants were on fire if I lost you."

"Well, let's try and avoid that then," I say. "I don't want to lose you either."

"Good. It'd be very pathetic. I'm talking begging."

"Really?"

"Oh, yeah. Your skin is so soft here." He rubs his thumb over the indentations of my spine. And you smell good."

"It's just lotion."

"Hmm." He licks over the dimples above my ass, following it up with a nip of the teeth. Making a shiver run down my back. Next, cunning fingers are tugging my panties low enough that they go into freefall and hit the ground at my feet. "Get rid of them, Anna."

"My panties?"

"Yeah."

I do as asked, stepping out of them and kicking them aside. For a butt-cheek health check followed by an apology, we sure are moving to the sexing stage of things pretty fast. Though considering one of us doesn't have our pants on, it was bound to happen.

His hand slides over my belly heading south and oh yeah. This is good. I could have sworn I wasn't the least bit turned on two minutes ago. Tension and anger and worry had me wrapped up tight. But now I need it. I need him. To assure me everything's okay. That we're still together and intact after that bullshit outside.

"Turn around," he says, sounding impatient.

I don't need to be asked twice. A dining chair is dragged out of the way and the edge of my ass is set on the table. His gaze is heated and expression determined. Like getting access to me up close and personal is all that's on his mind right now. Like being with me is all he wants and God knows I want to be with him too. He doesn't get off his knees and my dress is soon rucked up to my waist at the front too. Then it's all I can do to hold on as he positions my legs over his shoulder and makes merry with my girl parts.

"Fuck," I mutter at the first flick of his tongue against my clit. "You're so good at this."

"Customer satisfaction is very important to me."

"As long as your client base is limited to me, that is fine and dandy."

He chuckles and licks over my labia. He sucks and nips and pauses every now and then to graze his stubble against the sensitive skin of my inner thighs. A flurry of kisses is placed on my mound, then he's back at it again, fucking me with his tongue. I never know what he's going to give me next. It makes it hella exciting. When he adds a finger to the mix, pumping it in and out of me, I can't keep my eyelids open any longer. It's all too much. Too good.

Two fingers stretch me, coaxing me higher. Crude wet noises and the scent of my sex fill the air. He barely needs to rub over the back of my clit with those clever fingers and my body is already shaking. I come with very little coaxing. That spectacular high taking me over. It's kind of embarrassing how easy I am for him. How ready to give it up I am each and every time. It's also kind of awesome.

"Condom," I say, voice weak and breathy.

"On it."

After carefully untangling himself from my legs, he

sprints for his bedroom. I've never seen a man move so fast. The hard-on tenting the front of his gray sweatpants leave very little to the imagination. It's spectacular.

In no time at all, he's stripping off his tee and pushing down his pants, rolling the prophylactic over his swollen dick. His skin and his tattoos, his smile and his taste, everything about him works for me. At the sight of him, my heart feels too big for my chest. Like something's either gone very wrong or very right in there. It's just some mad infatuation. An all-consuming crush. And that's okay, it's fine, I just can't think about it anymore right now.

We're both clutching at each other, mashing our mouths together for the messiest kiss in history. And it's all so wonderful and frenzied and necessary. He slams his cock into me and oh hell yes. So good. We both moan in delight. Since I'm doing my best to cling to him like a howler monkey, he picks me up and stumble-walks us both to the nearest wall. This way we can stay smooshed together for the duration.

"Okay?" he asks, panting.

"Yes."

And no more is said. With one strong hand under my ass and the other arm wrapped around my back, he nails me into the wall. I hide my face in his neck and do my best to hold on. It's so urgent and all consuming. The need to get as physically close to him as I possibly can. I want to slide beneath his skin and wander through his mind. Know him better than I know myself. And none of these thoughts are the least bit sensible or cautious, but I can't help it. I'll worry about that later. The hard length of his dick surges into me, filling me to capacity again and again. My world is the heat of his body, the scent of his skin, the feel of him surrounding me and inside of me. The way he grinds the base of his dick against my clit and brushes over something fucking fabulous inside of me. Everything is tensing once again. My tummy tightening and thighs clasped tight around his hips. It surges up my spine, lighting up my whole world as I come again. Leif grunts and shoves his cock in deep, hips surging against me as he comes too.

Our limbs are locked around each other. Sweat and other bodily fluids on our skin. Ever so slowly and carefully, he takes us to the floor. And there we lie, sprawled out over each other.

"Holy shit," he mumbles against the side of my head.

It takes me a minute to catch my breath. "Adrenaline from the fight."

"Maybe. Or it might be just you. I can't get enough."

I brush some stray strands of hair back from his gorgeous face. Except he's beautiful inside and out, this man. And there's that weird and unfortunate heat and expansion inside my rib cage again. Honest to God, I could stare at him forever and it still wouldn't be long enough.

"Anna, baby . . ." he says in a low voice. His gaze is so warm and intense and oh my God. Everything. He's looking at me like I'm everything and it's too much.

"Hmm?"

"I, uh—"

"What do you feel like for dinner?" It's out of my mouth before I've even given it any thought. Safe neutral territory. Not that he was about to make things weird or anything. I'm probably being oversensitive or not sensitive enough or something. Or just somewhat deranged, who am I kidding?

"Dinner?" he asks, raising a brow.

"You're right. I need to get ice for your eye first." I crawl off of him and stand, smoothing down my dress and hunting for my panties. "You deal with the condom and I'll go in search of medical aid."

"Okay," he says. And if anything, he sounds sort of bemused. Whatever.

Nothing is wrong, I just came twice and it's a beautiful summer night. I empty a tray of ice into a kitchen towel and hey, presto. A couple of ibuprofen would be a good idea too. Meanwhile, Leif is back up on his feet and fetching two beers out of the fridge while being at least half dressed, which returns a little of my sanity. Though every time I look at him or hear his voice or enter his general vicinity I go a bit crazy. He shouldn't have such an effect on me. It's unnerving. Emotions are so wrong. They're dangerous and they can hurt.

Which is when I see them on the side table. A vase overflowing with flowers. Daisies, lavender, lilies, carnations, and roses. They're beautiful. All I can do is stare. "Where did they come from?"

"Huh?" he asks, flopping onto the lounge. "Oh. Yeah. I picked them up on my way home earlier. Mom is all keen to meet you, by the way. I don't think you're going to get out of going to family dinners for long. She's way overexcited."

"Really?"

"Come on," he says, holding a bottle of beer out to me. "If you're a good girl, I'll let you play nurse."

To this, I say nothing. But I do take the seat and the beer

and hold the ice to his poor wounded eye. I also hand over the pills.

He winces, the smile falling away. "At least I broke the fucker's nose."

"Never again."

"Which I will never do again because violence is wrong, even though he started it and deserved it."

I take a sip of beer. "Thank you."

"Like I was saying, Clem and Ed were singing your praises at dinner and now Mom is all hyped up to meet you. Hope that's okay."

"Ah, sure."

He smiles encouragingly.

"You know, as long as she understands . . ."

"What?"

"That we're . . . that it's early days and we, um . . . well, you know . . ."

"Sure," he says eventually, putting me out of my word-stumbling misery.

"Okay. Great."

"Clem mentioned she and Tessa had asked you to hang with them."

"Yeah?"

"You never mentioned," he says, gulping down some beer. "They like you a lot. Apparently they want to incorporate you into their girl gang or something. Secret handshakes may be involved. I'm not sure what the process is exactly."

"That's very kind of them."

"But it's not what you want?" he asks.

"No. I didn't say that."

"You're just holding back. Being careful." His gaze is gentle. "It's understandable."

"Is it?" I ask. "In some ways it feels cowardly. Like I'm putting my life on pause again."

"Trust takes time."

I frown, and my gaze darts back to the flowers and oh shit. He definitely saw that.

"You're not into flowers." It's not a question, it's a statement. "Never mind. Next time I'll get you something else."

"They're beautiful."

At this, he just blinks.

"I love them. I'm just a bit surprised because I thought we weren't sort of really being serious like that, you know?"

He gently pushes my hand holding the ice away from his face. "Anna, I was just thinking of you and wanted to make you smile. They don't have to mean anything if you don't want them to."

"And meeting your parents?"

His eyes go wide. "Huh. Okay."

"What?"

"You're freaking out."

"I am . . . I am not freaking out. It's just all a bit sudden."

He laughs.

"Why are you laughing?" I ask, voice tense.

"Sudden?" he asks with that damn eyebrow raised in query again. "No, come on. We live in each other's pockets, Anna. This is not sudden."

"Well, it is for me."

"You're kind of in denial then." He licks his lips. "You're holding back with me too."

I don't know what to say.

"I have been making a concentrated effort to woo you for a while now. Please tell me you've noticed."

"We were taking things slow."

He wrinkles his nose. "Sort of, but not really."

"What do you mean?"

"Look, you've been through a lot. I get it. And I'm all about you taking your time and feeling safe. But, baby, we live together, work together, and sleep together. I don't see how we could be any more together if we tried," he says, stopping to take a breath. Like he's trying to be patient, but right now it's costing him. "If me buying you flowers or you meeting my folks is upsetting then we'll put it off for now. But don't tell me that absolutely nothing's going on here between us, please. I don't think my heart could take it."

I just stare. And hold my beer and the ice.

He takes another deep breath and lets it out slow. "Maybe I'm a bit on edge after the whole Ryan thing. This isn't something we should be fighting about. Everything will be fine, okay? I'm going to take a minute and cool off, all right?"

"All right."

And he gets to his feet, goes into his bedroom, and doesn't come out again that night.

CHAPTER TEN

L EIF HAS ALREADY LEFT FOR WORK WHEN I WAKE IN THE
morning. I slept in due to staying awake half the night
listening for him. Because he never did come back out of
his room. Maybe he fell asleep. Maybe he's sick of my shit. I
just don't know. And everything I thought to say stalled on my
tongue long before I worked up the nerve to knock on his door.
Possibly he just needed some space. It happens. I'd have to be a
needy, pushy bitch to interfere with him having said space. Or
maybe I'm a coward. It's a hard call. So we haven't talked since
he accused me of holding back on him.

The truth of it is, I am. Of course I am. I'm fucking terrified
of where this is heading and if it's going to emotionally wreck
me like the divorce. What if Leif meets someone else and likes
her better? What if he decides I'm too much trouble? And if
that isn't a self-fulfilling prophecy then I don't know what is.
Dammit.

I spent a good part of the night listening to the unbroken
quiet of the condo, staring at my bedroom door, and gnawing
my heart out. If there was some sort of world record for worrying, I'd have been a sure contender last night. And the truth

is, Leif deserves better. I just have to figure out how to say it right. How to retain some pride and not burst into tears. Little things like that.

I wasn't supposed to be working today, but there's no way I can wait until tonight to talk to him. We're sure as hell not resolving this over the phone. After a good long shower, I throw on some jeans and a dressy white boho blouse with embroidery. Put my hair up in a stylishly messy bun and apply some makeup. An effort that hopefully says I want to be attractive to him and care about how I look. If he could take one look at me and fall at my feet, that would great. I am not, however, holding my breath. Hopefully the makeup will also cover my red eyes and any and all dark circles. Maybe I should bake something to take with me. Use that as my excuse for stopping by. Only waiting any longer to see him might actually kill me. Because when I walk into the tattoo parlor and he looks up and sees me, that's when it's going to happen. That's when I'll know. When my nerves will be put to rest. From that look I'm going to be able to tell where we are. If we're irretrievably broken or if I'm just being overdramatic. Fingers crossed for the latter.

Banging on the door happens just as I'm slipping my purse over my shoulder. It has to be Ed or Clem, because anyone else would have rung the buzzer on the outside of the building. Only I'd have expected both of them to be at work by now. Maybe Clem has a day off and wants to do something. In which case, I'll say yes. After stopping by to see Leif, of course. But I'll stop letting my anxiety rule me and I'll take a chance. Perhaps if I stop pausing and putting up walls then we can become great friends. Who knows?

Only it's not Clem standing outside the door. It's an older

man with salt-and-pepper hair and a flannel shirt sitting open over a tee. Greasy jeans and battered sneakers complete the look.

"Do you know me?" he asks before I can think to say anything.

"Do I know you? Um. No."

"Are you sure?"

"Do you know *me?*" I ask, bewildered and well beyond weirded out. "Where did we meet?"

"No. Pay attention. Really look," he insists, stepping closer. When he was already much closer than I liked. His face is lined and his eyes messed up somehow. It's the pupils. They're like pinpricks. "*Look.*"

"I'm looking."

And that's when I see it. The lump beneath his shirt, tucked into his jeans. My father used to have a gun in the house for security. Though he always kept it locked up tight. It might not be a gun hidden beneath this man's clothes, but what the hell else would it be?

"You don't recognize me at all?" he asks, hot breath stinking in my face.

"No. Not at all."

"You're sure?"

"Yes."

He waves on his feet a little. Whatever drugs he's taken, it's hitting him hard. "You better not be lying. It'll be real bad if you were lying."

"Absolutely. I am not lying. I swear." Except I am lying because now that I think about it, he is kind of familiar. The old dude looking at Mom at the café yesterday. And maybe he was sitting in his car outside during that whole fight with Ryan as well. Only he had sunglasses on that time. But I've definitely seen this man before. Not that I let it show on my face. I hold myself rigid, ready to attack. Not that I know a damn thing about attacking. I do have my keys in hand, however, with the pointy tips sticking out through my fingers. Maybe I can jab him with one in the throat or eye. If he makes a move, I have to do something. Defend myself somehow. My heart is pounding and sweat breaks out across my back.

"You don't want me to have to come back here," he says, going heavy on the threatening. "Neither of us want that."

"No," I agree. "Neither of us want that."

"Nothing about me is familiar?"

I shake my head.

His hands hang restless at his sides, and he reaches up to tug on his shirt self-conscious like, only his hand sits there waiting. Then he slips his fingers beneath the tee, touching the weapon, making contact. Next he raises the shirt a little to let me see. Yep. Definitely a gun. A compact black pistol that would kill me just fine. My gaze is stuck on the thing. And he's obviously made his choice. He's going to shoot me. Why would he show it to me otherwise?

This is the end of me and this time there'll be no second chances and I'll never get to say goodbye to the people I love. My family and Briar and Leif. Because I do love him even if I didn't realize right up until this minute when I'm most likely breathing my last breaths. It's crazy and maybe a little reckless and sort of impossible. But it doesn't make it any less true.

"All right," the man mumbles, letting the hem of his shirt drop back into place. "That's good."

My whole body is shaking and my throat is painfully tight.

"Don't forget now," he says simply, then turns and walks away.

The front door slams shut in the wind behind him. I don't know what makes me move to follow. Some strange burst of courage or curiosity. But I watch through the front glass door as he climbs into a silver sedan parked at the curb. The front corner of the car is crumpled and scratched to shit. As if it'd been in one hell of an accident.

My breath stops in my throat.

One hell of an accident. Just like the accident that rolled my car and caused Leif to crash. And Leif said it was a silver sedan that first time we talked. I remember it clear as day now.

"Holy shit," I mutter, amazed. Before I can open the door and sneak outside to see the license plate, my brain kicks in with a very valid point. Thank God. Because that man still has a gun and is very obviously unhinged and under the influence. The dude also kind of threatened to kill me. Let's not forget that salient point. "Security cameras," I say, still talking to myself, as if saying it out loud makes me more likely to listen to myself. "There are security cameras out front of the building and they catch the street. Leif said so. Don't go out there. Just stay put. Okay."

Thank God I listened to my better judgment for once.

It takes hours for the detectives to get here. Then they have to contact the building super and get him to hand over the security footage and so on and so forth. Leif bursts into the condo just as they're leaving. I have never been so happy to see someone in my life.

"Anna, what the hell?" he says, wrapping me up in a tight hug.

"You got my text?"

He cups my face in his hands. "The one that said you'd like to talk to me sometime soonish? Yeah. Then your mom called and told me to get my ass home pronto."

"Oh."

"Do you think maybe if it's an emergency like someone threatening to kill you, you might call the shop direct next time?" he asks in a gentle though still chiding voice. "I don't look at my cell when I'm with a client, okay?"

"Okay. That makes sense." I take a moment to think it through. "I don't think my brain was working quite right after the surprise of it all. I wanted you here, but I . . ."

"You what?"

"I just wanted you here," I admit, throat feeling choked again.

"I'm here, baby. I'm here. You're kind of spun out, huh?"

"Just a little," I admit, sliding my arms around his waist. My hands are still shaking a little and giving them something to do helps a lot. "They have his name, and they know the car. They're hoping to go pick him up now. I'll feel better once he's in custody."

"I bet."

"Never had anyone threaten to kill me before."

"Let's hope it never happens again."

"I can't believe he came here and did that," I say, voice full of fear and wonder. "If he hadn't, no one would have ever known he caused that accident. What an idiot."

"Drugs can make you paranoid as all hell. Part of his mind

probably thought you were just waiting to bring down his whole world or something." Leif rests his cheek atop my head. "When I find out who let him in the building, I'm going to have some stern words with them."

"Yeah." Just listening to his heart beating strong and steady against my ear makes me feel better. "Oh, by the way, I'm sorry about last night and I love you."

The man freezes.

"Okay?"

"Are you in serious shock or anything?" he asks carefully.

"No."

"You sure about that?"

"I can admit when I'm wrong," I say, somewhat churlishly. Just because.

"Yeah, it was more the other thing you said." He rubs a hand up and down my spine with brisk, sure movements. "The second thing."

"Oh, that." I sigh. "Well, when your life flashes before your eyes for probably the second time in a year, it clears away a lot of the bullshit and debris."

"That makes sense."

"I was neither looking to fall in love with someone right now nor particularly wanting to, but here we are and I'm done lying about it. To myself and to you."

"You know I was going to tell you last night?" he asks, pulling back to show me the sly smile on his gorgeous face. "That's why you freaked out and started babbling about dinner, right?"

"Maybe. All right, yes. I just wasn't quite ready to hear it."

"I had it all worked out and everything. You would've been the first woman I've said it to in about a decade."

"I'm sorry."

"It's fine," he says. "I wasn't angry with you, exactly. A bit frustrated, perhaps. I get why you'd want to take your time and it's perfectly understandable. Just needed to get my thoughts in order and shit. Then the meds and the general excitement of the day and all kicked in and I fell asleep. With all of the fucking we've been doing lately I may have needed it. You're very demanding."

"That's a very valid reason. But I hated sleeping apart from you. My brain may have been spinning wildly out of control without you."

"Let's not do it again, then." He smiles again. "I do love you, you know?"

"I know." And I'm smiling too. In fact, I'm grinning like a lovesick fool.

"Good."

"Saying I love you and getting into fights." I make a humming noise. "I think I'm a bad influence on you."

"Not even a little."

He presses his lips against mine, soft and sweet. It's a kiss so perfect it scatters the memories of any that came before. And if this is the man I get to kiss for the rest of my life, hot and heavy or soft and sweet, I'll be very happy indeed.

EPILOGUE

"**I**'M NOT SURE ABOUT THIS," I SAY, SWISHING THE SKIRT on my blue evening gown. Without a doubt, I am in full-blown princess mode.

"It's definitely not the sort of thing you should rush into." Clem's mouth flatlines in concern. "We can just pack all of this up . . ."

"Huh?"

"You know, give you more time to think it through."

Tessa nods. "She has a point. Big life decision happening here."

"Oh, no," I say, lifting the bodice on the strapless gown just a little. Nobody wants any nipples making an appearance at inopportune moments. Or at least, not too early in the evening. "I was talking about wearing this over-the-top dress as opposed to say jeans or something. Not about the other thing. We're full steam ahead on that front."

They exchange relieved glances. And fair enough too. We've only spent the last hour decorating the condo with candles and rose petals. It looks like St. Valentine exploded in here. Add the champagne chilling in the ice bucket and the mood music playing over the speakers and we are good to go.

"Mostly I was just wondering if a more relaxed feel with the wardrobe would be better," I explain. "Guess I'm just nervous. About everything. What if he doesn't like it?"

"He's going to love it. Now kick off your heels," says Briar over FaceTime. She couldn't get away from New York due to work, but wanted to participate in the moment.

I do as told, stopping to stretch my toes afterward. It's grounding, having the cool polished wooden floorboards beneath my feet. Suddenly it feels like I can breathe again. "Oh yeah. That's better. Good call."

Briar raises her glass of wine to me. "You've never really enjoyed wearing heels."

"Does anyone?"

Tessa shrugs. "Eh. Depends on the occasion. Just don't ask me to run in them."

And then it happens. Keys rattle in the door and Leif walks in, eyes going wide as the romance of the room smacks him upside the head. His cheeks are pink from the ice-cold wind undoubtedly blowing outside. There's a good reason I've got the heat cranked up to make wearing this somewhat scanty dream of a dress okay.

Clem's brows jump. "You're early! He's home early!"

"We're out of here." Tessa grabs her hand and they head for the door, squeezing past my boyfriend to get gone, closing the door behind them with a "Good luck!"

"You've got this," says Briar. "Don't let your anxiety get the better of you. Enjoy the moment and do your thing."

"Thank you," I say.

Briar gives me a saucy wink and hangs up.

"What's going on?" Leif tosses his leather jacket over the back of a chair, giving me a good look-over in the process. It's crazy, how the sight of him still makes me swoon. How butterflies go wild in my belly when he gives me that certain look. "Did I forget an anniversary or something? Why are you dressed so fancy, baby?"

I smile. "It's a secret."

"Huh."

"I will tell you all in my own good time, however. I'm a giver like that."

"Okay then." He gives me a lopsided grin that honest to God makes my knees weak. This man. Happy sigh. "You look beautiful."

"Thank you."

"One of these days I'm going to surprise the shit out of you and turn up in a suit."

"You'd look awful pretty in a suit. Of course you look awful pretty in anything. Or nothing. I'm a lucky woman."

He just grins.

"Why don't you do the honors and pour the champagne?"

"On it." He crosses to the bottle and the waiting glasses. "You know, the last time you were dressed like that was your happy divorce party going on six months ago now."

I slump oh so gracefully onto the sofa, accepting my glass of bubbly. A bit too much running around for one day maybe. Though the overall effect of all of our decorating the place is gorgeous and my friends were happy to help. It's nice to have new and awesome friends. I like it a lot. "It hasn't been long since all of that, has it? I mean it feels like we've been together a long time, but we haven't really. Everything about us being together used to worry me so much."

"But not anymore?" He sits beside me, slinging an arm around my bare shoulders and drawing me close. The motive for this becomes obvious when he takes a moment to peek down the front of my dress for various reasons. All of which make me smile.

"No, not anymore."

"Good."

"I'm happily living my best life and I hope you are too."

"You bet I am," he says.

"How was work?"

"Good. Art was in getting his children's signatures on his calf muscle."

"He's a nice man."

Leif smiles. "He is. He said to say hi."

"That's nice. Gosh darn you're handsome."

"I find you awfully fetching too, Anna. Especially all dressed up like you are," he says. "Though I also like you a lot naked with your hair all rumpled and sleep in your eyes. I'm easy for you like that."

"Why thank you, kind sir. I put extra effort in because I wanted to make something out of tonight. A surprise something." I couldn't keep the answering grin off my face if I tried. So instead I take a sip of booze and get my thoughts in order. Hours have been spent in front of the mirror preparing for this speech, but the words still feel like a jumbled anxious mess on my tongue. "It's more than just attraction between us, you know? A lot more. You're my best friend, Leif. You're smart and kind and you mean everything to me. Life is better with you."

His gaze warms at the words. "Thank you."

"The last few months with you have been the best. And that's wild given how bad the ones leading up to it were. So I pulled on my big-girl panties and made a certain phone call today . . ."

He cocks his head. "Did you now?"

"Yes." I nod. "I rang your lovely mother and asked for her blessing to ask you to marry me."

Beside me, the man freezes. "You did what?"

"You heard me."

"Yeah, I did . . . I'm just surprised." He blinks. "Anna, baby, I thought you didn't want to get married again. You were pretty damn against the idea if I remember correctly."

"No, I didn't. Because I didn't see how I could ever trust someone like that again. Didn't know if I could ever feel that secure and happy, you know?"

"That makes sense."

"But I do feel that way. With you."

He exhales. "Wow. I'm so glad to hear that."

"And I was wondering if maybe you feel that way with me?"

The corners of his lips edge up again. "I most certainly do. But we can keep going on as we are if you're not comfortable with more."

"That's what I'm telling you, my love. I *am* comfortable with more. I'm comfortable with all of it when it comes to you."

He just shakes his head in wonder. But he still hasn't said yes. This is an important point.

"And when we were doing our rewatch of *The Twilight Saga* last week, I happened to notice how you kept watching me out of the corner of your eye during the wedding scenes," I say.

"Anna . . ."

"And that look on your face when Bella was walking down the aisle. It made me think that maybe I'd been a bit selfish ruling out marriage."

"I told you," he says. "I had something in my eye. That's all."

"Sure. Okay. It's a beautiful vampiric cinematic moment and no one would blame you for getting caught up in it." I set my glass aside and turn to face him more fully. His expression is grave, his focus entirely on me. I grab hold of his hand, holding on tight. "But also, as I just explained, my reasons for ruling it out didn't really add up anymore."

Nothing from him.

"So I'm asking you to marry me."

Still nothing from him.

Oh, God. My hands are a sweaty mess. "If you would like to do that maybe?"

"Anna." His throat moves as he swallows. "Are you certain that's something you want as opposed to being something you'd tolerate to make me happy? Because it's kind of a big deal. We'd be legally bound together."

"I know."

"Even if we ran off to Vegas and kept things on the down low, it'd be a big deal amongst our family and friends."

I frown. "Yes. I know. People will have opinions. That's what you're hinting at, right? Most will be delighted, but not necessarily everyone. Thing is, as I said before, I don't care. I refuse to care. I love you and I don't mind who knows it. At the end of the day, this is about you and me and fuck everyone else."

"Fuck everyone else?"

"Yes."

He blows out another breath. "So that's what the candles and rose and fancy dress are about?"

"It felt like it should be a big moment, you know?"

"I know." His smile is gentle and sweet now. "And I appreciate it. I just don't want you doing something to please me that you're going to regret."

Now I'm really losing my nerve. Mostly on account of me running out of words. Maybe he's trying to let me down gently. Maybe I was wrong and we're not there yet. But no. Leif loves me and I'm certain of that. I trust him. Though maybe this isn't what he wants at all. A wedding and marriage and things changing again so soon.

"You're frowning," he says. "Stop that."

"Of course I'm frowning, you haven't said yes yet."

"Huh?" he asks, brows drawn together. "Oh. Yes, of course. I thought that was obvious. I'd love to be your husband. It'd be an honor and a duty and a pleasure."

"Thank goodness for that," I mumble, my shoulders deflating.

"You were worried?"

"Just a little."

He laughs, planting kisses on my forehead. "Please. I'm a fool for you. There's no way on earth I'm not marrying you given half the chance. So long as it's what you really want."

"It really is." I rest my cheek against his shoulder with a smile. "I promise."

His big hand cups my face and maneuvers me into position for a long and deep kiss. A soul kiss. My absolute favorite. The scent of him and taste of him and just everything about him is the best. He still goes to my head like fine wine and he always will. Therapy has helped a lot with his nightmares. It's also helping me get a grip on life, the universe, and everything. Neither of us will ever be exactly what we were before the accident, but that's okay. Starting over taught me a lot, but without a doubt, he's one of the amazing things to come out of everything. One of the things I'll never stop being grateful for. While I know I could live without him, that I could have rebuilt my life alone if I had to because I'm strong enough and good enough, that I didn't have to is a blessing I'll never take for granted.

Just when I thought it was impossible, he made me believe in love again. I really am a lucky woman.

Continue reading for a sneak peek of

Fake

Chapter One

He slunk into the restaurant mid-afternoon wearing his usual scowl. Ignoring the closed sign, he took a booth near the back. No one else was allowed to do this. Just him. Today's wardrobe consisted of black jeans, Converse, and a button-down shirt. Doubtless designer. And the way those sleeves hugged his biceps . . . why, they should have been ashamed of themselves. I was this close to yelling "get a room."

Instead, I asked, "The usual?"

Slumped down in the corner of the booth, he tipped his chin in reply. For such a tall guy, he sure went out of his way to try to hide.

I said no more. Words were neither welcomed nor wanted. Which was fine since (A) I was tired and (B) he tipped well for the peace and quiet.

Out back, Vinnie the cook was busy prepping for tonight, his knife making quick work of an onion.

"He's here," I said.

A smile split Vinnie's face. He was a huge fan of the man's action films. The ones he'd made before hitting it big time and taking on more serious dramatic roles. Him choosing to visit the restaurant every month or so made Vinnie's life complete. Especially since the restaurant, Little Italy, was the very definition of a hole in the wall. Not somewhere generally frequented by the Hollywood elite. Meanwhile, I was less of a fan, but still a fan. You know.

"Get him his beer," Vinnie ordered.

Like I didn't know my job. Sheesh.

He was busy with his cell by the time I placed the Peroni in front of him. No glass. He drank straight from the bottle like an animal. Just then, a woman in a red sweater dress and tan five-inch-heel booties strode in through the front door.

"I'm sorry, we're closed," I said.

"I'm with him." She headed straight for his booth and slid into the other side, giving the man a dour look. "You can't just walk out, Patrick. You're going to have to choose one of them."

"Nope." He took a pull from his beer. "They all sucked."

"There had to be at least one that would do."

"Not even a little."

She sighed. "Keep this up and you'll be obsolete by next week. Beyond help. Forgotten."

"Go away, Angie."

"Just another talented but trash male in Hollywood. That's what they're saying on social media."

"I don't give a shit."

"Liar," she drawled.

I wasn't quite sure what to do. Obviously they knew each other, but he did not seem to want her here. And she really wasn't supposed to be here. Vinnie had okayed after-hours entry to only one person. On the other hand, if I asked her to leave, she'd probably sic her lawyers on me. She looked the type.

The woman spied me hovering. "Get me a glass of red."

"She's not staying," countermanded Patrick.

Angie didn't move an inch. "They were all viable options. Pliant. Young. Pretty. Discreet. Nothing weird or kinky in their backgrounds."

"That might have made them more interesting."

"Interesting women is what got you into this mess." The woman frowned, taking me in. Still hovering. One perfectly shaped brow rose in question. "Yes? Is there a problem?"

Now it was Patrick's turn to sigh and give me a nod. He was so dreamy with his jaw and cheekbones and his everything. Real classic Hollywood handsome. Especially with his short light brown hair in artful disarray and a hint of stubble. Sometimes it was hard not to stare. Which is probably why his personality tended to scream "leave me alone."

I headed for the small bar area at the back of the restaurant to fetch the wine like a good little waitress.

"We shouldn't be discussing this here," said Angie, giving the room a disdainful sniff. Talk about judgy. I thought the raw brick walls and chunky wood tables were cool. Give or take Vinnie's collection of old black-and-white photos of Los Angeles freeways. Who knew what that was about?

Patrick slumped down even further. "I'm not going back there. I'm done with it."

"This isn't safe." Angie looked around nervously. "Let's—"

"We're fine. I've been coming here for years."

"You just got dropped from a big-budget film, Patrick," she said, exasperation in her tone. "The industry may not find you bankable right now, but I'm sure gossip about you is still selling just fine. This week at least."

A grunt from the man.

"The plan will work if you let it. Everything is organized

and ready to go. It's the perfect opportunity to start rewriting the narrative in your favor." She jabbed a finger in his direction to accentuate the word "your." The woman clearly meant business, and then some.

I set the glass of wine down in front of her and returned to my place at the back of the room, polishing the silverware and restocking the salt and pepper and so on—all the jobs best performed when things were slow. And while it was nosy and wrong to listen in on other people's conversations, it wasn't my fault the room was so quiet that I could hear everything they said.

"None of them felt authentic," he said, stopping to down some more beer.

The woman snorted. "That's because none of them are."

"You know what I mean."

"When you first came to me you said you wanted to become a star, make quality films, and win an Oscar. In that order," she said. "As things are at present, you may be able to resurrect your career to some degree through the indie market. Pick up roles here and there and slowly build yourself back up. But that's going to take years and you'll likely never be in the running for the golden statuette. You can kiss that dream goodbye."

Patrick ran an agitated hand through his hair.

"You worked your ass off to get this far," she said. "Are you really going to give up now?"

"Fuck," he muttered.

"Liv is busy saving her own ass and you're unwilling to set the record straight. Not that anyone would even necessarily believe you at this point. So our options are limited." She picked up her wine, taking a delicate sip before wrinkling her nose in distaste. Since it came out of a box, that wasn't much of a surprise.

She'd only asked for a glass of red; she hadn't specified quality. "I know you were hoping it would all die down, but people are still talking. And with social media how it is, this was the worst possible time to get caught up in a scandal. However, there is hope. We can still salvage things if you'd just work with us. But we need to act now."

Patrick declined to respond.

It had been all over the internet a month ago. Photos of him leaving Liv Anders's Malibu residence at the crack of dawn. And it was clearly a morning-after picture. Totally a walk of shame. He'd been all disheveled and wearing a crumpled tux. Liv being half of Hollywood's current darling couple was part of the problem. Along with Patrick and Liv's husband, Grant, having just done a movie together and supposedly being best buds. That Patrick had spent his earlier years dating a string of models and partying hard didn't help matters either. His reputation was well established. Headlines such as "Patrick the Player," "Walsh Destroys Wedded Bliss," "Friendship Failure," and "Not So Heroic Homewrecker" were everywhere. Maybe it had been a slow news week, but the amount of hate leveled at him was surprising.

Of course, there had to be more to the story. There always was. But Liv was seen weeping in a disturbingly photogenic fashion as she and her husband walked into a marriage counselor's office the next day. And the pair had been hanging off each other on the red carpet ever since. Meanwhile, Patrick's name was mud. Worse than mud. It was toxic shit.

It could all be true. He could indeed be a trash male who thought with his dick and behaved in a duplicitous and manipulative manner. I'd dated my fair share of dubious men, so it wouldn't exactly surprise me. And plenty of assholes had been publicly outed recently. Men who used their fame and power for evil.

But this all just felt more like gossip.

First up, there'd been no actual evidence that this wasn't two consenting adults doing what they wanted behind closed doors. Patrick hadn't taken any wedding vows and Liv hadn't made any accusations of mistreatment. In fact, Liv hadn't said anything at all. Patrick and Grant being best buddies, though . . . that was a hell of a betrayal. If it was true.

"Fine. I'll do it," he said, his voice rising. "But not with any of them."

"Patrick, we've been interviewing for weeks to find those three alternatives for you," she said. "One of them must be tolerable if not perfect."

"She doesn't need to be perfect. She needs to be real."

"Real?" asked Angie with some small amount of spluttering. "Give me strength. That's the last fucking thing we need right now."

The bell pinged out back. Vinnie gave me a wink and nodded to the waiting dish, Penne Ragu and Meatballs with Parmesan. It smelled divine. As the size of my ass could attest, I loved carbs and they loved me. And what was more important, jeans size or general happiness?

Vinnie took pride in his food. Pride in his restaurant. It was one of the reasons I liked working for him.

"They're all waiting. Come back to the office," said Angie as I reentered the room.

"No."

"Patrick, how the hell else are you going to find someone? If word of what we were doing got out . . ."

"That's not going to happen."

The woman looked to heaven, but no help was forthcoming. "If you won't choose one of them, then who?"

"I don't know," he growled.

As stealthily as possible, I set the meal down in front of him. Invisibility was an art form. One I didn't always excel at when he was around. It's not my fault. Attractive men make me nervous. So of course my fingers fumbled over the silverware and the fork clattered loudly to the table.

"Her," he said, staring right at me. Possibly the only time we'd made direct eye contact. It was like looking into the sun. I was all but blinded. The man was just too much.

"What?!" Angie shrieked.

I froze. He couldn't be referring to me. Not unless it was in the context of a "you are totally clumsy and not getting a tip today" sort of thing.

"You cannot be serious," Angie all but spluttered, looking me over, her eyes wide as twin moons. "She's so . . . average."

"Yeah," he agreed with enthusiasm.

Wow, harsh. I was pretty in my own way. Beige skin and long, wavy blond hair. A freckle or two on my face. As for my body, not everyone in this city had to be stick thin. But whatever. The important thing was, I was a nice person. Most of the time. And I was kind. Or at least, I tried to be. Personal growth can be tricky.

"Enjoy your meal," I said with a frown on my face.

"Sit down a minute." Patrick gestured to the space beside him in the booth. "Please."

Instead, I crossed my arms.

"I want to talk to you about a job opportunity."

Angie made a strangled noise.

"I have a job," I said. "Actually, I have two."

"What's your name?" he asked.

"You've got to be joking," hissed Angie. "They'll never believe it."

"Norah," I said.

"Hey, Norah. I'm Patrick."

"I know," I deadpanned.

He almost smiled. There was a definite twitch of the lips. For someone whose charm-laden devil-may-care grin had graced billboards all over the country, he sure knew how to keep that sucker under wraps. "How'd you like to make some serious money?"

"Don't say another word until she's signed an NDA." With a hand clutched to her chest, Angie appeared to be either hyperventilating or having a heart attack. "I mean it!"

Patrick just sighed. "Angie, relax. I've been coming in here for years and she's never once put anything on social media or taken a creeper shot. I bet you haven't told a soul about me, have you, Norah?"

So I respected his privacy. So sue me. I also kind of liked hearing him say my name. Him just knowing it was a thrill. Definite weakness of the knees. "You seem to enjoy the anonymity."

"Even stopped that girl from asking me for an autograph."

"The owner's daughter," I said. "She's still not talking to me."

Another almost-smile. There was definite amusement in his pretty blue eyes.

Fake

Angie downed the last of her boxed wine in one large gulp.

Patrick and I stared at each other like it was a contest. Who would dare look away first? Me, apparently.

"What's the job?" I asked.

"I'd need you full time for a couple of months," he said.

"A year, and live-in," corrected Angie.

Patrick cringed. "Six months and live-in. No more."

With a wave of her fingers, Angie relented.

I cleared my throat. "Um, doing what, exactly? Being your gofer or an assistant or something? Or do you need like a house-keeper or a cleaner?"

"No," he said, calm as can be. "I want you to be my fake girlfriend."

Purchase at your favorite online retailer to continue reading.

PURCHASE KYLIE SCOTT'S OTHER BOOKS

Fake

The Rich Boy

Love Under Quarantine

Repeat

Lies

It Seemed Like a Good Idea at the Time

Trust

THE DIVE BAR SERIES
Dirty
Twist
Chaser

THE STAGE DIVE SERIES
Lick
Play
Lead
Deep
Strong: A Stage Dive Novella

THE FLESH SERIES
Flesh
Skin
Flesh Series Novellas

Heart's a Mess

Colonist's Wife

ABOUT KYLIE SCOTT

Kylie is a *New York Times* and *USA Today* best-selling author. She was voted Australian Romance Writer of the year, 2013, 2014, 2018 & 2019, by the Australian Romance Writer's Association and her books have been translated into fourteen different languages. She is a long-time fan of romance, rock music, and B-grade horror films. Based in Queensland, Australia with her two children and husband, she reads, writes and never dithers around on the Internet.

www.kyliescott.com

Facebook: www.facebook.com/kyliescottwriter

Twitter: twitter.com/KylieScottbooks

Instagram: www.instagram.com/kylie_scott_books

Pinterest: www.pinterest.com/kyliescottbooks

BookBub: www.bookbub.com/authors/kylie-scott

**To learn about exclusive content, my upcoming releases and
giveaways, join my newsletter:
kyliescott.com/subscribe**